# VALENTINE'S ROSE

*The Bride Train Series*

## E.E. BURKE

Cover Design by Erin Dameron-Hill
Train photography by Matthew Malkiewicz

Published by E.E. Burke
ebook ISBN: 978-0-9969822-4-5
Paperback ISBN 978-0-9969822-5-2
www.eeburke.com

# THE BEGINNING

*Taken from an advertisement posted by the Missouri, Fort Scott &
Gulf Railroad in Eastern U.S. newspapers*

## EVE, FIND YOUR ADAM IN THE GARDEN OF
## THE WORLD!

Single young ladies of good reputation desiring to emigrate
west for the purpose of marriage may apply to the Young
Ladies Immigration Society for free travel to southeastern
Kansas where hardworking settlers are eager to make your
acquaintance and become steadfast husbands. Applicants
must be free to wed, preferably between the years of 18 and
25, without deformities, debts or other encumbrances. Dance
hall girls, circus performers, and soiled doves need not apply.

*May 2, 1870, Centralia Settlement, Eastern Kansas*

Outside the saloon, a train whistle wailed.

"Women!" The cry went up in unison. It echoed off framed walls and bounced around a smoke-filled room.

Denim-clad settlers slammed their glasses down on top of upturned barrels. Other men flung empty bottles to the sawdust-covered floor, grabbed straw hats, and bolted out the entrance, past a door that had yet to be hung.

Constantine Valentine gathered the cards, picked up his winnings, and rose from his seat. He didn't require a woman at the moment, although he could afford one if the urge struck now that he'd broken his losing streak.

As he stepped outside onto the loose planks forming a makeshift sidewalk, a stiff Kansas wind slipped down the back of his shirt. He turned up his coat collar.

According to a dirt farmer, this settlement—Val wouldn't call it a bona fide town—had purposely been situated on the highest point in the county. From here, one could see for miles.

Nature had drawn a line roughly along the route taken by the railroad with timbered lands to the east, and to the west, a vast grassland, which, according to the knowledgeable farmer, topped "the richest soil on God's green earth."

Val didn't have much interest in soil or in anything green for that matter, save greenbacks. He had no use for grassland, but the men around here clamored for it, so he felt certain he could easily sell the deed he'd tucked into his pocket—if he could divert attention away from the women. That seemed unlikely at the moment.

A shiny locomotive puffed as it pulled a long train behind it that stretched out of sight on the grassy prairie. Hitched behind the tender box was a single passenger car followed by a long line of freight cars and flatbeds loaded with ties and rails.

As the steam engine approached the station, the whistle sounded a second time, then an ear-piercing screech of brakes.

The eager throng cheered as they splashed across the road, oblivious to the ruts filled with mud and manure. They elbowed and shoved, engaged in a jostling competition to be first to the railroad platform. More men appeared from a nearby general store. Several others leaped from their wagons, leaving harnessed mules in the middle of the street.

"I grant you, females are scarce out here, but is there always such a commotion over the arrival of members of the fairer sex?" Val asked the stocky saloon owner who'd limped outside to join him at the open door.

The Irishman leaned his shoulder against the frame and folded his arms across his chest. "The railroad is bringing in a new shipment."

Val tried to make sense of O'Shea's odd remark. He

couldn't be talking about... "Do you mean to say, they are *shipping* women?"

"Brides."

Even stranger.

"That must be a new line of business for the railroad," Val observed. "Delivering brides."

"*Bribes*, more like. To get us to agree to their terms for settling our land disputes. They're offering special incentives to men who sign up to tie the knot." O'Shea lifted his arm to grip an invisible rope, tilted his head, and grimaced, making it clear what he thought of the institution.

"Enterprising of them. How did they convince the women to come out here?"

"They posted advertisements in newspapers. Promised them a free trip west to the land o' plenty." O'Shea harrumphed. "Kansas has plenty, all right, plenty of horny devils."

The railroad whistle sounded again, its shrill tone rising above the lusty shouts of the men rushing to meet it.

Val felt a twinge of pity for those poor, unsuspecting ladies. Then again, the only women who would take such an offer were bound to be destitute, ruined, or ugly. "Are you certain it is *brides* they are delivering?"

"Ah, well, we got whores. Maybe not enough to go around, but that ain't the type of woman these fellows want. They're yearning for wives. They want to raise families."

Val nodded. He wouldn't admit it out loud, but he understood. He'd come to a point in his life where the idea of domesticity didn't make him cringe. However, it didn't bear dwelling on at the moment because he wouldn't consider marriage until he'd made his fortune here in America. Then he could return to England and get on with his life. He'd select a wife well-endowed with a substantial dowry.

In front of the train platform, mounted soldiers stood

guard. The brass buttons on their blue coats winked in the midday sun.

From inside his coat, Val withdrew a slender cigar—his last—and enjoyed a smoke, along with the entertainment across the street. "The railroad hired an army to guard the brides? That seems extreme, even for Americans."

"President Grant sent troops out here on account of the riots," O'Shea explained.

"Riots? Whatever for?"

"Those of us who fought their war came out here in good faith, staked out claims under preemption, then the government sold all the land to the railroad. Now the new owner wants five times as much as it's worth." The burly Irishman spit into the mud, showing his contempt. "You'd know all about wealthy landowners who charge tenants too much, being as you're an English lord."

"I am not a lord," Val corrected. He hadn't inherited the title or his father's wealth. The only land he owned was what he'd just won in a poker game.

The locomotive ground to a halt. It heaved a smoky sigh. Along the side of the passenger car, feminine faces appeared at the windows. Some looked alarmed, others downright frightened. None of them appeared to be in a hurry to depart the safety of the railcar.

The panting throng of men surged forward, but the soldiers intercepted them before they could reach the platform. Only a conductor, baggage handler, and an official of some importance were allowed near the train.

Besides Val, the railroad official was the only other gentleman wearing a proper suit. He lifted his hands as if to roll back the Red Sea. "Keep your distance. Don't crowd the ladies."

O'Shea lifted his chin. "That's Mr. Hardt, our new land agent. The one before him got whipped and run outta town. He was a molly, though. Don't know what to call this one."

"Matchmaker?"

The Irishman chuckled. "Maybe we'll put an apron on him before we toss him on a rail."

It didn't sound as though Mr. Hardt would be around for long either.

An over-eager farmer slipped past the soldiers. As he climbed onto the edge of the platform, the strapping railroad agent shoved him off, sending him ass-first into the mud.

"We'll proceed in an organized fashion—"

Shouts and whistles drowned out the rest of the official's remarks.

At last, the women exited the train.

Val counted heads. Only a dozen. "Do you know how many men signed up for brides?"

"Least a hundred, I'd wager," O'Shea answered.

These sex-starved men had rioted over land prices. What would they do in light of a limited supply of women?

"More soldiers might be in order."

The ladies huddled together, remaining close to the car as if they might dash back inside should things get out of hand.

Amid the feminine company stood the tallest lass Val had ever seen. The color of her hair remained hidden under a drab scarf that reached past her shoulders, but even from a distance, he could tell she had the distinct pale complexion common to the British Isles. He couldn't distinguish the color of her eyes, but he'd swear they were green.

The shapeless garment she wore gave the word *ugly* new meaning. That might be why she'd wrapped her upper half in a plaid shawl. It didn't help. The hem of her skirt needed another three inches to cover her petticoats, not to mention her ankles. And what was she wearing on her feet? Those looked like her father's boots. Regardless, even an ill-dressed, gangly gal like that one could find a husband among undiscriminating suitors—him being the exception.

He'd only noticed her because she had to be one of the few women who wouldn't have to crane her neck to meet his eyes. Beyond her remarkable height and coloring, she had little to recommend her.

"Poor things. They must've run out of luck," O'Shea murmured. "Wonder if they'll last?"

"That one in the middle looks like she might stand a chance." Val buttoned his coat as the wind picked up. "Think I'll get a better look."

He started across the street, circling the crowd, then moved in the direction of the frame building adjacent to the brick depot. When he reached the opposite sidewalk, he doubled back as far as he could go, given the throng. From this point, he could easily see over the other men's heads. One of the advantages of his extraordinary height.

The women remained close together near the steps leading up to the platform. Consoling each other perhaps? Several men acted as baggage handlers and removed the trunks and cases.

A strong wind whipped at the Amazon's scarf. In the next moment, an invisible prankster ripped it away.

The land agent bolted after it and missed.

Val watched the scarf flutter in his direction, dancing over the crowd, tantalizingly out of reach for the men leaping to claim it. Val had but to raise his arm to snatch the prize out of the air. Exultant, he waved the cloth at the owner.

Streamers of hair the color of flames whipped across her face. She pulled them away. Upon spotting him, she broke into a grateful smile.

He grinned in return, then realized he was acting like a fool over some woman he'd never see again. After he returned her scarf.

Val examined the article that had captured every man's attention. It was nothing more than a large square of washed-out blue, repurposed from a dress or shirt. He rubbed the worn fabric between his fingers. The tall lass ought to have a nice bonnet or hat to set off the color of her beautiful hair. One of these yokels should purchase one for her.

"When do we start the bidding on picnic baskets?" yelled a man from the center of the crowd. His remark drew more laughter than was warranted.

Mr. Hardt didn't find the remark amusing. He stood with his feet braced, like a sailor anticipating the next swell. "There won't be any picnics," he announced. "We have more requests than brides. We'll hold a lottery later today over at the courthouse."

Shouts of outrage and more than a few curses peppered the air. Had armed troops not been present, the all-male crowd might've rushed the platform.

The women's expressions ranged from shocked to furious. No one had told them their husband's names would be drawn from a hat.

Val couldn't decide whether he admired the man in charge for being clever or despised him as an unfeeling cad.

"There's more." The now-unpopular land agent pitched his booming voice above the noise from the crowd. "Only men with registered claims will be considered. A list of qualified candidates is posted outside my office." Hardt didn't allow time for questions before he escorted the stunned brides-to-be off the platform.

The soldiers formed a protective wall between the ladies and the grumbling crowd.

Val kept to the front of the swell. He paused when the ranking officer rode by on a spirited bay. Before the next soldier blocked his view, the railroad agent strode past with his face set in stone.

Several ladies followed single-file, taking mincing steps on a wide plank that had been laid over the mud. Val scarcely took note of the women, being focused on looking for the tall girl. When she passed, he would step in and hold out her scarf so she could take it.

He heard her clomping before he spotted her. She walked with an odd gait in a pair of boots that didn't fit well or pained her.

As she drew near, Val stepped forward, inserting himself in between two mounted soldiers, and held out her scarf.

Her head swiveled. The moment their eyes met, hers went wide with surprise.

He'd been right, only her eyes weren't just green, they were the pale, verdant color of spring leaves.

She reached for the scarf and slipped off the plank.

Val caught her arms when one of her boots sank into the soft mud. She clung to his shoulders, gazing at him with an awestruck expression. Had she not expected him to assist her?

"Get back," shouted the soldier immediately behind her. He appeared to be talking to the other men who were trying to crowd in.

At any rate, Val didn't loosen his grip. But the girl tried to scramble backward, apparently thinking the order was directed at her. Her boot made a sucking sound before it popped off.

Three soldiers closed ranks around them and the parade came to a halt.

Val slipped his arm around the young woman's waist—a surprisingly slender waist. He steadied her as she hopped back to the sidewalk. She perched on one foot like a heron.

He plucked her boot out of the mud. "Put your hand on my shoulder for balance. If you'll pardon the liberty, I'll slip this on so you won't risk falling again."

When he knelt, her bemused expression shifted to one of horror.

"Oh-oh no, sir. You don't hafta kneel for me."

Her thick Irish accent took Val aback, though he might've expected it. Her ragged dress and plaid shawl looked like something worn by the peasantry. The uncharitable thought fled when he looked into her eyes and saw her soul. She was as pure and innocent as he was debased and wicked.

"Do me the honor," he urged her.

This time, she didn't hesitate. Her elegant fingers curled over his shoulder. At her touch, desire flickered.

There was something about a woman's hands, and this woman had beautiful hands. Likely her feet, which were presently covered by wool stockings, were also long and slender and just as pale.

Val grasped her ankle. The sensuous flicker ignited into a flame. His face grew warm at his uncontrollable reaction. What in God's name was wrong with him? He hadn't gotten hard this fast the last time he'd been with a woman wearing nothing *but* stockings, and silk ones at that.

Her hand trembled.

Val clenched his jaw, hating that he'd unsettled her, and gently guided the girl's foot into the muddy boot before lacing it up. He secured the loose laces on the other boot.

"Wouldn't do if you tripped again. I might not be at your side the next time to catch you." He hoped his jabbering distracted her from noticing his overheated condition.

The railroad agent stepped between two soldiers and frowned at Val as though he'd done something wrong. "What's going on here?"

Val came to his feet, slowly. He thought it apparent what was *going on*, but maybe the surly agent hadn't been paying attention. "This young lady slipped. I assisted her."

He drew the scarf out of his pocket and presented it to her.

She took it, rather gingerly. "Th-thank you," she murmured.

Val had little patience with women who affected shyness. In most cases, flirtatious pretense. But this girl's blushes weren't accompanied by a fluttering of eyelashes. Nor did her tongue-tied reaction come across as feigned.

She might be flustered because she'd experienced the same reaction he had when he touched her foot. Or something more in line with what a lady would feel at the pull of attraction. Whatever the reason for her rosy glow, he found it enchanting.

He executed a formal bow. "A pleasure, my lady."

"All right, the damsel is saved. Let's get moving." Mr. Hardt flicked a speculative gaze over Val before giving a nod to one of the soldiers who motioned him away.

Val found the entire exchange insulting. However, there was little point in making an issue of it. He'd done his good deed.

Before he turned away, he made eye contact one last time with the young woman. He considered wishing her luck in finding a husband and then changed his mind. Being bartered off to these rough men who didn't have the least idea of how to treat a lady would not be considered lucky by any stretch of the imagination.

He focused his attention on moving through the crowd and down the street without becoming the same brown color that stained everything and everyone.

Time to get back to business. At Mr. O'Shea's saloon, he'd find an interested buyer, quickly sell the deed he'd won, and get the hell out of this Kansas mud-hole.

**R**ose Muldoon stood on the makeshift sidewalk and stared after the retreating gentleman with amazement. He didn't talk or look like those other men who'd rushed the train with their tongues hanging out. Her handsome, black-haired rescuer stood apart. And not just because he topped the tallest men by several inches, but because of his manner and attire. That black suit fit him so perfectly it had to be custom-made.

*Imagine.* A high bloke like him bowing to someone like her.

He slipped between two horses and headed off in the opposite direction, making his way through a crowd of men still milling about in the street. According to Mr. Hardt, the railroad agent, close to two hundred unattached settlers lived in the area. They must've all come to town to meet the train.

Did the handsome gent live 'round here? Would he be taking part in the drawing?

The brisk wind ruffled her skirt. She tightened the knot on her shawl to prevent it from blowing away again. The wind wasn't cold as much as a nuisance, trying to slip its fingers beneath her petticoats like that old coot Donohue. That fine gentleman hadn't tried to pinch her behind the knee when he took her ankle to slip the boot back onto her foot. No, he'd been ever so gentle and polite. If he'd felt her trembling, he didn't show it. Just thinking about his hands brought on another heated flush.

One of the mounted soldiers rode up next to her. "Ma'am? You need to keep moving."

Rose fell in behind the other women and shuffled along on the rickety boards. A pair of men's boots had been among the charity items collected by the church and were the only ones that came close to fitting her. T'was a good thing she had on stockings so the gentleman hadn't seen her blisters. That would be almost as humiliating as falling on her face in the mud in front of him, which she would have done if he hadn't caught her.

A smaller man would've dropped her or lost his balance. The tall gentleman acted like she weighed nothing. When he'd put his arm around her, he'd been reaching down, not up. And he hadn't looked at her like she was a freak. If the Almighty had shaped a man to fit her, He couldn't have made one more perfect. But had she opened her mouth to talk to him? Oh, no. Instead, she'd behaved like a *hickjop*. The only thing worse would've been to drool on the Englishman's polished black boots.

Rose cast another longing glance over her shoulder. He'd disappeared into the air like a faerie prince. Or more likely, he'd gone into one of the many saloons. Wherever he'd gone, it didn't matter to her. If the fine bloke were in the market for a wife, he'd want a more refined lady. One like the pretty widow in front of her, whom she'd met on the train.

Susannah Braddock might decide she liked the handsome gentleman. Too embarrassed to ask outright, Rose posed a question.

"What sort of man do you favor, Susannah?"

"Not one I draw out of a hat," she replied over her shoulder. "I'll choose my own, thank you."

Such confidence might work for Susannah, who had a fair face and tiny form that turned men's heads, along with the bonus of a good education and not bearing an Irish name. Rose had none of those things in her favor.

"What if the blokes don't agree to be chosen?"

"Any man you select would be honored, I'm sure."

Rose wasn't so sure. Not because she didn't have pride. That was the problem. She had too much pride. Back home, she'd gotten propositions but no decent offers. At least the men in Kansas were willing to tie the knot. But she had better put that fine gentleman out of her mind, or be ready to meet with disappointment when he didn't show up for the drawing, or worse if he did and got matched up with someone else.

Susannah winged open a fringed shawl and cloaked her seven-year-old son against her side when young Danny started to wander.

Rose smiled, recalling the countless times she'd tried to keep her little brother out of the mud. It rarely worked, given Willy's fascination with puddles. Susannah's energetic young son had the same mischief dancing in his eyes. The two boys might have become fast friends if they'd ever met.

They never would. Not in this life.

Rose's heart constricted at the memories. For a time after that awful fire, her grieving had been so intense she hadn't thought she would survive and didn't want to. Father McCarthy had suggested she take advantage of the railroad's offer and go find herself a husband. Have her own family. It wouldn't replace the one she'd lost, but it might ease some of the pain and the aching loneliness. With a corner of her shawl, she wiped away tears.

*There now, no more crying,* her mother would've told her. *We all have our crosses to bear, and yours is no heavier.*

Susannah slowed to look over her shoulder once more and her brow furrowed with concern. "Rose, never fear. That officious railroad agent can't force us to take part in this travesty. We will appeal to the authorities."

Rose wasn't sure what *travesty* meant, and she didn't see how pleading with those in authority would help. That sort didn't care about people like her. "What would they do? Before we appeal, let's get a look at who shows up for the drawing."

Her rescuer's image popped into her head. His lips were as perfect as those on the statue of St. Michael, and a square jaw added strength to his lean, aristocratic features. Ah, he had the loveliest eyes. A fascinating blend of blue and gray, light as crystal.

"There won't be a lottery. Not if I can help it." Susannah's firm reply burst the daydream. "We must have the freedom to choose whomever we want. Not just the men Mr. Hardt says are qualified or those he picks from a hat. What gives him the right to limit our choices?"

Some women had limited choices, regardless. But Rose didn't correct her friend on the matter because it wasn't in her nature to argue. She offered an observation instead. "Mr. Hardt, he's not that different from other men. They all think they're put on earth to be in charge."

"I won't argue that." Susannah hugged her son closer. "Which is why it is up to us to teach them differently."

Rose imagined her father's explosive reaction if her mother had announced he wasn't in charge. "If you don't mind, I'll be leaving that task to you."

"You don't agree, Rose?" The question came from the woman behind her.

"What I think doesn't matter," Rose replied, hoping to avoid an argument.

"Of course it does," Susannah returned with vehemence. "What we all think matters. Just because we're women doesn't mean our opinions don't count."

"Tell that to Mr. Hardt." Charm LaBelle projected the reply around Rose's right side. The top of her head didn't even reach Rose's shoulder.

What Charm lacked in size she made up for in personality, even in the way she dressed. She stood out like a bright-feathered bird. She'd been all the way to California and back to New York and had spun wondrous tales during the train ride.

The Englishman might prefer a well-traveled woman like Charm. Except he'd have to lift her to kiss her.

"That uncharitable land agent is leading us along like the Pied Piper," Charm muttered. "I wonder if he remembered to collect our trunks."

Rose glanced down at the donated carpetbag she carried. She hadn't needed a trunk or a suitcase to contain all she owned in the world—another dress, also donated, night clothes, and a rosary Father McCarthy had given her. She only had her mother's shawl because she'd wrapped up in it when she'd left the apartment early that fateful morning, just before dawn, to collect clothes to be washed. When she'd returned, the building had been ablaze.

"Oh, good heavens!"

The morbid thoughts invading Rose's mind disintegrated at Susannah's outburst.

"Mr. Hardt, please slow down! Our legs are not as long as yours."

She'd called out several times to tell him he was walking too fast. The mounted soldiers riding alongside them hinted at the reason—the rambunctious crowd.

In New York's Sixth Ward, men were even more numerous and just as rowdy. Being whistled at and ogled didn't seem as strange as disembarking in a town that had been plopped down out in the middle of nowhere.

From one end to the other was only a couple blocks, if you could call a muddy thoroughfare lined with wobbly planks *blocks*. The depot appeared to be the only sturdy building, the rest being constructed out of rough wood shingles, including a general store, a grocery, and three gin houses, what they called *saloons*. It was surprising there weren't more, what with all these men and no mothers, sisters, or wives to keep them out of trouble.

Mr. Hardt had assured them the fellows would settle down now that women were here to offer a *civilizing influence*. He couldn't possibly believe twelve women could civilize all these men.

Rose would settle for the one who didn't appear to need civilizing.

Ah, that was wishful thinking. She sighed longingly then put the foolish notion out of her head. She'd come out here to marry one of those *hard-working settlers* Father McCarthy had told her about. He hadn't mentioned the advertisement saying anything about English gentlemen.

### ❧ 3 ❧

**R**ose's feet burned from blisters all around, by the time she reached the end of the second block. It wasn't the walking. She walked all the time and all over. Maybe it hadn't been wise to give up her only shoes for a pair of sturdy boots that Father said would be more useful on a farm. She'd find some rags to stuff inside them after Mr. Hardt stopped the parade.

The railroad agent stopped in front of a two-story clapboard house with a fresh coat of white paint. Didn't look like a courthouse, as he'd mentioned. He went off to speak to the officer in charge of the soldiers. When he returned, he ushered his charges up a set of stairs leading to a porch that wrapped around the front.

Rose squinted up at a sign posted over the door. One of the words was *House*. She couldn't make out the first word. *L-a-g-o-n-d-a*. It could be a name.

She'd only gotten as far as reading simple words before she had been forced to leave school to help her mother take in more washing and mending. Her days had been filled with scrubbing other people's clothes and her nights with caring for younger siblings while her mother continued to work. Schooling had been a luxury they couldn't afford. The night before the fire, she'd argued with Mam about how unfair it was for her to have to give up her education and not her brothers, and she'd said some hurtful things.

Her throat tightened and her eyes began to sting. She would give up anything, everything, to go back and apologize and embrace her family again. Perfect or not, they were all she'd had in the world and she'd loved them fiercely. But they were gone now. So she had best stop dwelling on the past, accept the fact that she was alone—

"Miss Muldoon?"

Hearing her name snapped Rose out of her daze. She came back thoughts of the shabby apartment where she'd lived to a grand entrance with paneled walls and rich furnishings. She looked in confusion at the man standing in front of her.

Mr. Hardt's hard features had remolded into what might be called concern. What had she done or said to worry him? Even stranger, he appeared to have brought the women he had taken charge of into his home. "Are you unwell?" he asked.

Rose couldn't recall the last time she'd been ill. "No, sir."

"You should sit down." Susannah was around the same age as the other women, but she had stepped into a mother hen role she seemed to find most comfortable.

Rose allowed it because she liked Susannah, not because she needed another mother. And she wasn't all alone. She had new friends. "I'm fine. Just tired."

"It's been a long day," Susannah murmured, looking pointedly at Mr. Hardt.

He smoothed his hand over his wavy black hair and hung his hat on a hook attached to what appeared to be a high-backed chair. A looking glass was mounted near the top.

Rose gazed at her wide-eyed reflection. A hall tree was what they called it. She'd seen them on occasion when she'd delivered clothes her mother had mended for wealthier customers.

A gray-haired lady chatted amiably with some of the other women. She ushered everyone into a front parlor. The woman looked too old to be Mr. Hardt's wife, though she could be his mother.

"Is this yer house?" Rose asked him.

His confused frown made her blush. She'd guessed wrong and made a fool of herself. "Mrs. Fry runs the Lagonda House," he answered. "It's the only hotel in town."

Rose didn't want to admit she had never been in a hotel. She hadn't ridden a train before either, until a few days ago. She hadn't ventured beyond Five Points for most of her life.

"You ladies can freshen up here before we go to the courthouse," he said in a loud enough voice for everyone to hear.

All conversations stopped.

Susannah Braddock narrowed her eyes at the railroad agent. He stared right back at her with no reaction. She spoke softly to her son, instructing him to go wait in the parlor with the others while she had a word with "the nice gentleman."

As soon as Danny was out of earshot, she dropped the sweet smile. "Are we to assume this is where we'll remain until such time we choose to wed?"

"Until later this afternoon, yes," he returned smoothly. "You do recall signing an agreement that you are willing to be married."

Susannah's chin went up. "I have every intention of marrying. When I am ready to do so and with someone I select."

Challenging a stubborn man wouldn't get her anywhere.

Rose knew this well, having lived with the stubbornest man ever created. Her father.

She hugged her shawl, debating whether she ought to step into the fray. She didn't want to contradict her friend or offend the railroad agent, but this concerned her too. She'd been able to reason with Da. Convincing Mr. Hardt to compromise seemed an easy enough task.

"We're all in agreement about marrying, sir. What Mrs. Braddock is wanting, I think, is a little time to get used to the idea." Rose held the railroad agent's gaze, which wasn't difficult as they stood eye-to-eye.

Most men were uncomfortable with her being the same height—or worse, taller. Mr. Hardt had no visible reaction. His thoughts remained shuttered behind eyes as dark as the deep blue sea.

*When all else fails, try a friendly smile.*

"If you was to grant us a night's sleep, we'd all be chirpy and looking our best in the morning for them coves you picked out."

The railroad agent blinked. "Coves?"

"Gents."

"Ah." He pressed his lips together. She might've thought he was trying not to smile if he'd shown a hint of humor earlier. "You've missed your calling, Miss Muldoon. As a diplomat."

Another fancy word. He used a lot of them.

"What's that?" she asked.

"Some would call them peacemakers."

He'd meant it as a compliment.

Rose gained a little confidence. "You're agreeable, then?"

Susannah heaved a sigh. "I'm relieved to hear it. We'll need some time to settle in and get our bearings. Tomorrow or, better yet, after a few days, we can meet our suitors in an acceptable situation. A social would be a proper venue."

The railroad agent frowned. What Susannah suggested didn't sound offensive to Rose, but there was something about the Boston widow that rubbed Mr. Hardt the wrong way.

"The last time we arranged a social, the Land League used the distraction to wreak havoc. No socials." He sounded firm on the matter.

"We can manage without," Rose broke in. "If we might have a look at those men on that list you mentioned?" The way her luck had been going, the handsome gentleman wouldn't be involved. If he was, would she be able to guess his name?

"Yes, that would be much better than forcing us to take part in a game of chance."

Susannah meant well, but Mr. Hardt wouldn't be calling her a *diplomat*.

The oncoming storm started in his eyes. Rose had seen her father lose his temper, and that's what he looked like, right before the gale struck.

"This isn't a game, Mrs. Braddock. You all came out here to be married, and so you shall be, as soon as possible. I'm willing to allow you to remain here one night, at the expense of the railroad, but you had better be ready first thing in the morning. We'll hold the drawing at ten."

"What makes you think we'll agree to a lottery?" Susannah braced her hands on her hips in a challenging pose. "There is no need to rush."

Mr. Hardt crossed his arms over his chest. "Yes, ma'am, there is a need. We must put an end to these endless disputes over land ownership, which means assigning claims as quickly as possible. And our policy states the first assignments go to married men."

Disputes, claims, it all sounded like nonsense to Rose. What did make sense, though, and what she should've expected, was the motive. These marriages were just transactions to the railroad. Business and, in the end, money. Things were no different out here than at home.

After the initial stab of disappointment, she stated the obvious. "Daub their palms, you mean. Only, we're to be the grease, and you need to apply it quick."

"Grease?" Susannah asked.

Was it not clear enough?

"So he can get whatever it is he wants from these men," Rose explained.

Her friend's confusion turned to shock. "He's using us as bribes?"

"*Brides*," Mr. Hardt said firmly. "Miss Muldoon misunderstood." He held Rose's gaze, daring her to contradict him.

He could deny it all he wanted, but she'd lived in Five Points where bribery was a way of life. And she wasn't as ignorant as he thought. But nothing would be gained by arguing with the high-and-mighty bloke. For the moment, she'd hold her tongue.

Susannah tipped her head to look up at the railroad agent. Her expression as she studied him implied puzzlement more than anger. "Is this true, Mr. Hardt? Is the reason you're in a hurry because you have to pay someone off?"

His face drew as taut as a bow string on a fiddle.

Rose sent her friend a warning look. Susannah had a way of asking questions that made them sound like insults.

"The longer we linger and allow you and the other ladies to become a distraction, the more likely there will be trouble," he replied in a tight voice. "Suffice to say, tempers are short. These men are restless. The sooner you're wed, the better."

Rose searched the agent's stiff expression, trying to interpret what was behind his guarded words. "Are you saying we're in danger?"

His features softened the slightest bit. She wouldn't have noticed if she hadn't been watching him closely. "No, Miss Muldoon. I wouldn't allow harm to come to you, to any of you. But part of my job entails seeing that you are matched up, and I intend to do that in an efficient and expedient manner."

And he was going about it in the wrong way. Being a *diplomat*, Rose didn't say that. She understood the situation. He needed them to get something he wanted. They needed him to get what they wanted. A deal could be struck. "It won't take long to pick out our husbands once we meet the fellows."

His black brows gathered in a frown more thoughtful than angry. "There are over a hundred men signed up for brides. The fairest way to match you up is to draw names."

"That's the quickest way, to be sure, but it's not fair to *us*."

He rubbed his forehead. His wasn't the only head aching. Plus, her feet hurt. "What do you suggest?" he asked wearily.

Susannah opened her mouth.

He responded by placing his forefinger over her lips. "Don't ask me to arrange a social."

She drew back, startled.

He'd done that to fluster her or to get her to shut up. Maybe both. Frustration didn't give him license to embarrass her. But he didn't act a bit regretful, nor did he offer an apology.

"Your suggestion, Miss Muldoon," he prompted.

Her suggestion? First, she had to come up with one. "The men on that list, why not let them come by here and call on us? One at a time, and we do our own choosing. That would be proper...and it's not a social."

Disappointment clouded his features. "Interviews could take weeks."

He'd expected her to come up with a better answer. That

was the best she could do, and it met his requirements. Mostly.

"But the *coves* would all get their chance and we'd all end up married like you want."

He shook his head. "I can't wait that long."

"*You* can't wait? This isn't about you—" Susannah stepped back with a look of alarm when the railroad agent raised his finger. Her rosy skin turned five shades of red.

She glared at him. "Miss Muldoon has a good idea, and I'm sure the others will agree. We'll meet with the men here, one at a time. Or not at all."

Rose sucked in a sharp breath. *Oh, Susannah. No.* Now was not a good time to teach this man a lesson about not being in charge.

"Very well," he said in a calm voice that sent a shiver down her spine. "Return tickets can be arranged."

He would send them back?

Rose shook her head. Her tired eyes stung. She couldn't return to Five Points. There was nothing to return to except crushing poverty, unbearable memories, and a bleak future. So many good men had died in the last war. Those who'd returned were either married, too damaged to consider, or uninterested in marrying a "giantess." Immigrating west had been her best chance at a decent life.

Her *only* chance.

Casting her pride aside, she grabbed Mr. Hardt's arm before he could walk away and seal her doom. "You want us to be married quick? Fine, then. I'll marry the first man who'll take me. Even if he's the next one who walks through that door."

## ❧ 4 ❧

After the hubbub surrounding the arrival of the bride train, the saloons had emptied out and the men who'd been drinking earlier were now gathering somewhere in the vicinity of the courthouse for the bride lottery. Val decided he'd wait at O'Shea's establishment until the drawing ended and the bachelors returned, thirsty for a land deal that didn't include marriage.

Even Mr. O'Shea's popular establishment had been vacated by every man except the owner. Rather than racing out to meet potential brides, O'Shea lavished his loving care on an ornately carved, mahogany bar. The impressive piece would be more suited to a London gentleman's club. Instead, it sat amongst the sawdust and cigar ashes, surrounded by barrels repurposed as tables.

O'Shea didn't lack for dreams, though he did lack one thing Val possessed. A titled heritage. However, without the benefit of an inheritance, a title was as useless in America as it was in England. Thankfully, Val's streak of bad luck at the card tables had ended and he possessed something of real value.

Val rested his arms on the shiny bar top and one foot on the brass rail. "I'll have my usual, thank you."

O'Shea glanced up. "Back already? I thought you'd gone to rescue that tall lass."

"Heavens, no. I am a knight errant."

"A what?"

"A wanderer, on a different quest, one that requires liquid assets." Val removed the deed from his pocket. "Would you know anyone who might be interested in purchasing this deed to a section of arable land?"

Amusement flickered across O'Shea's broad face as he set a glass in front of his customer and poured a precious shot of fine whiskey. "You ought to be aware of something before you try to sell that piece of paper. All the land 'round here belongs to the railroad. That'll include what you won."

Val looked at the signed deed and his stomach pitched. *No.* He couldn't believe he'd fallen for a hoax. "Are you saying this is bogus?"

"Oh, it's real, far as it goes." The Irishman stopped cleaning the bar and set the cloth aside. "But it's not worth anything until the railroad says so."

Val breathed with relief. "I understand the protocol. After I take care of some paperwork with the railroad, then I'll own it."

Laughter remained in O'Shea's eyes. "It's a wee bit more complicated than that. The railroad agent is assigning land first to the men who take part in their matchmaking program. Ned Jarvis, the bloke who bet the deed, plans to get himself a bride. Once he's married, he won't need that piece of paper. He's already registered and proved his claim. He'll just apply for a new deed from the railroad."

Heat flooded Val's face. "The damn rascal tricked me!"

"Looks that way." O'Shea grinned like it was the funniest

joke in the world. "But you aren't from around here. No reason you'd know. I wouldn't feel too bad if I was you."

Val didn't feel *bad*, he felt murderous. "How much is this land worth?" Was it worth risking a noose for wringing Jarvis's neck?

"That depends on who you ask," O'Shea returned, "Six dollars an acre, according to the railroad."

Val's jaw dropped in astonishment. "For prairie grass?"

The Irishman gave a philosophical nod. "Some might say it's worth lots more. Not for what's on the surface, but for what's underneath it. Coal."

A shiver ran down Val's spine. His family's fortunes had come from coal. Winning that hand of poker had to be a twist of Fate. Or what he preferred to call Destiny. He held the deed to land that could be worth a fortune—if he could gain the rights to it before the former owner cheated him out of it.

Val downed his drink and slapped a coin in front of the saloon owner. "I'll have a word with Mr. Hardt."

"Good luck with that."

O'Shea's chortles followed Val out the door.

He turned in the direction of an angry horde gathered in the street outside a building just beyond the depot. It wasn't a courthouse, so that had to be the land office.

Men quarreled and cursed. A fight broke out when one man attempted to get ahead of another. Those closest to the building were clustered around a news board mounted to an outside wall. Presumably, they were anxious to get a look at the list of *qualified* suitors. Either the railroad agent had not returned or he'd locked his door.

Val reined in his impatience. He'd find Hardt, demand to speak with him in private, explain how he'd come by the deed, and persuade the agent to give his request special consideration. They couldn't provide brides for every man with a valid claim.

One of the men near the edge of the crowd had been in the saloon earlier. Val recognized the dated frock coat pulled tight across the young settler's brawny shoulders. He'd paired the fitted coat with an aged waistcoat over plaid trousers and scuffed boots. Someone had given him bad fashion advice. That, or he was employed in a traveling medicine show.

"Excuse me, sir. Do you know where I might find Mr. Hardt?"

The man gave him a suspicious once-over for what Val thought was a polite inquiry. "You're that fellow who won the land from Ned Jarvis."

Was this one an interested buyer?

Val dismissed the temptation to offer the unfashionable yokel the deed in exchange for quick cash. He didn't appreciate being fleeced, and, quite selfishly, he wasn't ready to part with land that was possibly worth a fortune. "That's right." Val offered his hand. "Constantine Valentine."

The man's gray-blue eyes remained cool as he took Val's hand. "Arch Childers."

His grip was surprisingly firm, almost painful. His youthful features would place him in his early twenties, younger than most of the settlers, but few were over forty. It took youth and strength to carve a farm out of wild grassland.

"Could you tell me where I might find Mr. Hardt?" Val asked politely.

"You aren't from around here," Childers drawled.

Another astute observation.

"My ancestral home is in England," Val acknowledged.

Interest flared in the young man's gaze. "Are you a duke?"

Why did Americans assume all well-heeled Englishmen were dukes?

"My father holds a minor title. His lordship isn't a duke."

"Lord Jesus is the only lord I know."

"An excellent joke," Val said, wearily.

"Check the hotel." Childers pointed in the direction. "I reckon Mr. Hardt is holed up there with the women until the drawing this afternoon. He's posted a few soldiers outside. You might not get through."

Having successfully talked his way into an audience with royals, Val felt certain he could get past a few soldiers.

"I'll take my chances." Val touched the brim of his hat. "Thank you, Mr. Childers."

As he walked away, the young man called out. "They might let you in if you tell 'em it's *the Lord* calling."

Val gave a wave to acknowledge he'd heard. Someone, no doubt, appreciated the homespun humor. Mr. Childers, perhaps.

At the hotel, there weren't *a few* soldiers. Mounted troops surrounded the place. Mr. Hardt must have feared the unhappy settlers would storm the house, steal the women and string him up. Given the mood of that crowd at his office, his concern wasn't unfounded.

Val devised a strategy. He would stroll up to the hotel and pretend to be a guest. The soldiers might not stop him. The yokel's suggestion wasn't a bad one, and he could play that lofty card, if necessary. After all, he'd been trained for the role.

He squared his shoulders, put on his best lord-of-the-manor air, and got across the front porch before a private posted by the door stopped him.

"State your business, mister."

Officers and aristocrats had one thing in common—the presumption of superiority.

Val looked down his nose as he reached into his pocket and withdrew a card. He rarely used formal calling cards out here, many Westerners having never seen one. But at times like this, they came in handy. He held it out to the soldier. "Mr. Hardt is expecting me. Urgent business."

The soldier's gaze traveled over Val's impeccable attire. He barely looked at the card before he opened the door.

Val released a relieved sigh. He never thought he'd be grateful for learning how to be officious. He'd have to remember to thank his father.

As he stepped inside, his nose caught the subtle fragrance of women's perfume.

Mr. Hardt stood beside a hall tree with his attention focused on a short, curvaceous blonde. Towering over her was the young woman Val had assisted earlier. She'd pulled off that ugly scarf. With absent, almost self-conscious, movements, she attempted to tame wayward curls that had escaped a thick braid forming a flaming nimbus around her head. If she released her hair, the length might reach her waist.

Val conjured an image of the goddess with her tresses down, its thickness shielding her slender form. Nude, except for a pair of stockings.

The door shut behind him. His nerves jumped as the sound reverberated in the wood-paneled hallway. Before he could make sense of why this young woman had such a powerful effect on him, she turned her head and gasped like she'd seen a ghost.

Her reaction got the attention of the other two.

The railroad agent's surprise quickly transformed into displeasure. "How did you get in here?"

"I walked through the front door. You must be Mr. Hardt." Val strolled up as if he'd been invited. He didn't intend to get tossed out before he could open his mouth. Opting for respectful formality, he sketched a slight bow to the ladies. "Constantine Valentine, at your service."

The two women remained frozen, staring at him. Both

were attractive. To men starved for female company, they would be a veritable feast for the senses. It would be a miracle if the suitors didn't kill each other.

Val's gaze lingered on the statuesque redhead. Her crown reached his nose, which put her at close to six feet.

*Remarkable.*

He returned his attention to the stony-faced agent. "Excuse the interruption, but we have some urgent business to discuss—"

Hardt turned away. "Whatever it is, this isn't a good time. Come by my office later. I'll see you then."

The curt dismissal grated on Val's nerves. "This afternoon will be too late. By then, a mistake will have been made. One that will be difficult to correct."

The railroad agent frowned at him. "What mistake?"

Val reached inside his coat pocket. "This is a deed to land claimed by Mr. Ned Jarvis. He wagered it and lost. I understand you must assign the land to me before—."

"That's true. I don't see how it's urgent."

*Rude, impatient, with an annoying tendency to interrupt.*

Val continued in a polite tone. "I've been led to believe Mr. Jarvis plans to secure a bride and assert his right to this claim on that basis, which is why the matter is urgent. I respectfully request that you assign the land to me before he can perpetrate this fraud."

Hardt took the deed. He barely glanced at the paper. "Whose name is on it at this point doesn't matter. I won't assign land until after the weddings take place."

"But he signed over the deed, as you can see," Val pointed out, nicely.

"He might've signed it, but we haven't assigned him the claim. He can't transfer ownership. Being a foreigner, you wouldn't be aware of the legal intricacies."

"I have a firm grasp on American laws—and the loopholes."

"There are no loopholes in this case, Mr. Valentine. Married men will be assigned claims first. Do you happen to be married?"

Val held his temper in check. No small effort. "Not at present."

"You could be," blurted the flame-haired woman.

Her astonishing remark arrested the company in the hall.

Val's composure slipped and his jaw came unhinged. Had she just issued him a proposal?

The girl blushed then dropped her gaze to the floor. The rosy color rising in her cheeks made her fair skin glow. Despite her outlandish outburst, she gave the appearance of being innocent. If she wasn't, she was a fine actress.

The shorter woman nabbed her arm. "Rose, no. You don't know anything about him," she said in a harsh whisper. "Don't sacrifice yourself."

Rose pushed her friend's hand away. "Leave me be. I'm not goin' back."

"This is madness. He won't carry through with his threats," the other woman continued to plead. "He can't force us."

Before Val could decipher the drama, Hardt extended the deed. "I'll assign you the claim if you take this one—" He grasped the smaller woman's arm and dragged her in front of him. "Off my hands."

Her eyes went wide with shock. Then she twisted around, her gray skirts swirling and slapped the agent's cheek. In the hushed stillness, the blow resounded like a thunderclap.

With a furious cry, she tore free and rushed down the hall.

Val considered applauding. An excellent show and he hadn't even had to pay an admission.

The imprint of the offended lady's hand appeared on

Hardt's face as his complexion darkened. His jaw muscles worked as though he were grinding his teeth.

The lady named Rose came out of her daze. She turned to the railroad agent with her hands up, pleading. "Please, sir, don't be very angry."

Val discerned the reason for her worry and the urge to protect her gripped him. "If you've threatened these women—"

"Threatened?" Hardt faced him with a frown. "I don't threaten women. They signed an agreement. I've been tasked with matching them up. Some of them, like Miss Muldoon, are more cooperative."

By offering herself to a man she'd just met?

Val couldn't imagine why Rose Muldoon had cooperated in such a manner unless she felt pressured. "It doesn't appear they're pleased with your matchmaking methods."

"They'll be less pleased if riots break out," Hardt shot back.

He had a point. Since the women had arrived, the town had turned into a powder keg. These ladies represented the spark.

The process of *matching them up*, as Hardt had so crudely put it, required care, diplomacy, and a deft touch. Arranging marriages was clearly outside of his wheelhouse. It would be easier to feel sorry for him if he weren't so arrogant.

The land agent turned to the woman at his side. His harsh demeanor softened, the only hint he might possess a shred of humanity. "Are you certain about this one? I won't hold you to your offer to take the first man who walked through the door."

His cryptic remark elicited another warm glow on Miss Muldoon's cheeks. She gathered her tattered shawl and wrapped it around the upper half of her faded dress, perhaps assuming he'd questioned her because of appearance. At the same time, she held her shoulders back and lifted her head.

A pauper who carried herself like a queen.

Val's respect for her grew by leaps and bounds. It would almost be worth it to see his father's reaction when he brought her home along with a small fortune.

"I'm certain." She darted a questioning glance in his direction. "If he is."

What the hell was he thinking? He'd come in here to persuade Hardt to assign him a piece of land, not give him a bride. His future waited across an ocean in a different life and with a highborn lady. Not with a poor Irish lass, no matter how brave or beautiful.

"You cannot be serious." He'd addressed the comment to Hardt, but couldn't help notice her crushed reaction. "I meant that most respectfully. You see, I am not what one would call a *good catch*, despite appearances."

The land agent held out the useless deed. "Mr. Valentine, you may propose to Miss Muldoon now or you can get in line with the others and take your chances."

Val couldn't find his voice. This had to be the most outrageous thing that had ever happened to him, and he'd lived a fairly outrageous life. But if he walked away, he might as well bid adieu to the land and to a fortune that could save him.

He tugged at his coat sleeve while a standing clock in the hall ticked the seconds. Marriage would create complications. Strings that would have to be severed. He had no right to entangle an innocent girl simply because she was under pressure to marry.

A worry line appeared between the young woman's eyebrows, the same unusual color as her hair. Seeing her distress, and knowing he was partly the reason for it, he offered her an encouraging smile.

"You could find someone far better," he said softly with absolute sincerity.

She flashed a shy smile, as if he'd meant the comment to be amusing, then blushed and lowered her lashes. Her fingers tightened on the ends of the shawl.

All the signs were there. The young woman wanted him. Badly.

The responsive tightening in his groin took Val by surprise. Sex wasn't in the cards. If he went through with this sham marriage, he'd not leave her with a child to raise on her own. After he ascertained the value of the land and sold it, he would give her a generous portion, along with an annulment. Pretty Rose would be free to find another man to her liking or she would be well off enough to postpone a second marriage if she so desired. Looking at it that way, a brief, chaste union could be good for both of them.

"Very well." He dropped down to one knee and looked up —something he rarely did. "Miss Muldoon, would you do me the honor of becoming my wife?

## ❧ 5 ❧

The wedding was to take place *immediately*—or as close to it as possible. How this might be accomplished, Rose wasn't sure. The town didn't have a church or a priest within fifty miles. But Mr. Hardt had declared the front parlor of the Lagonda Hotel a sacred enough place, and the owner happily went to fetch a preacher.

Everything happened so fast it didn't seem real, and Rose wouldn't have believed it except for the tingling she still felt after her fine gentleman had taken her hand and asked for it. If he requested her heart, she would give him that, too.

"Constantine Valentine." She spoke his name under her breath to get the feel of it on her tongue. The fancy name suited him, but for some reason he preferred to be called Val, which was fine with her. She liked it and Val was easier to say.

Four of her new friends hurried her into one of the bedrooms where she was told to change into something fresh and clean.

Rose stripped out of the wool dress that had mud stains on the hem. With trembling fingers, she reached into her bag for the only other option. A black gown that one of the nuns had altered for her to wear to her family members' funerals.

"You wish to wear mourning attire for your wedding?" Susannah asked. "I certainly understand, although your groom may not."

"I-I don't have another," Rose stammered, blushing.

"I'll loan you something." Delilah, one of the other brides-to-be, fetched her suitcase and heaved it onto the bed. When she unbuckled the straps and threw them open, clothes exploded onto the coverlet. She pulled out a cream-colored jacket decorated with exquisite embroidery. "This ought to fit you. Then you can return it for me to wear at my wedding."

Rose gasped. What if she tripped and spilled punch on it? "Oh, that's too fine for me to—"

Delilah tossed the garment at her. "Put it on.

Before Rose could object again, Delilah retrieved another item. A bustled skirt made of pale, pink silk. She held it up and eyed Rose, then scrunched her regal nose.

"I'm sorry," Rose mumbled. "I'm too tall."

"Don't apologize for how God made you." Susannah took Rose by the arms and turned her around. "I think we can fix this."

What? Her extreme height?

"I don't see how," Rose bemoaned.

"We shall need an extra-long petticoat."

"My sister Hope has one," Delilah offered. "I'll go find her."

Rose tried to recall the other woman. Hope's skin had a warm, golden glow and her eyes were dark, almost black. Delilah's eyes were blue and she had a porcelain complexion, marred only by a scar on one cheek that might've come from a burn. Perhaps she'd gotten too close to a stove as a child. The two women didn't much look like sisters, but not all family members shared the same features. Among the Muldoon clan, only Rose had red hair and green eyes.

She tried not to cringe with embarrassment while Susannah found an extra corset. Something else Rose didn't own.

A moment later, Hope, the taller of the two sisters, showed up with a lacy petticoat. She helped Rose adjust it around her hips. The lace hem extended several inches below the borrowed skirt, almost to her ankles.

"It's very fashionable," Charm pronounced. "But you need pretty stockings and shoes."

Rose didn't think she could get any redder but the warmth in her face proved her wrong. "I'd never be able to squeeze my feet into your shoes. Nor shoes from any of you."

Susannah produced a pair of silk stockings. "Wear these and go without shoes for the ceremony. No one will say a thing."

"You'll need something to hold them up." Charm lifted her yellow skirts and removed a pair of bright red garters. "I can make do with another pair. I've got several."

Someone knocked at the door just as Rose drew on the garters.

"Mama, I picked flowers!" announced a childish voice.

"Thank you, Danny." Susannah gathered a handful of purple and blue wildflowers her son had collected, tied the dangling stems together with a ribbon, and presented it to Rose. "Every bride needs a bouquet."

Tears rushed to Rose's eyes and clogged her throat. "You are all being so kind and generous. How can I ever thank you?"

"We're your friends, Rose," Susannah said solemnly. "Friends help each other."

These women had done more than help. They'd saved her from abject humiliation and from offending her groom.

Rose stroked the smooth skirt. A rough cuticle caught on the fabric. She jerked her hands away, horrified she might've snagged a thread. Her hands were red and chapped. She couldn't ask her friends for gloves, which wouldn't fit her anyway, and they'd done enough for her. What could she do for them? "I'll be happy to do your laundry," she offered.

Charm sank into a chair in the corner and twirled a blonde curl with her forefinger. "I suspect your new husband will keep you too busy to think about washing clothes."

Susannah smiled. Hope and Delilah exchanged nervous glances.

Rose busied herself with checking the length of the skirts. She wasn't unaware of what men and women did together. Her family had lived in close quarters and she'd known from the time she was young that children didn't simply spring up out of the soil or drop from the sky. But knowing something and experiencing it was very different.

When men had approached her for favors, she'd been disgusted at the thought of their hands on her. But when Val touched her, her skin got tingly and her heart pattered faster. She looked forward to their wedding night with a mix of excitement and trepidation, mostly out of fear that she would somehow disappoint him.

He'd been so kind. He would teach her what she needed to know.

After she'd finished getting dressed, Susannah reworked her hair into tidier braids. "I don't know why we have to rush."

Rose had listened closely enough to understand her husband-to-be's general concern. "Val wants to claim his property before another man cheats him out of it. Mr. Hardt said we had to be wed before he'll sign off on the deed."

Susannah frowned as if the explanation didn't satisfy her.

For sure, Rose wasn't so slow she didn't understand that

Val had offered for her to get something else he wanted. Yet she felt convicted to defend him. "He's a kind man."

"I pray you're right. And you'll grow closer over time, as you work together and start a family."

Rose would pin her hopes on Val's kindness and Susannah's prediction.

Mr. Hardt was waiting in the front parlor with Val and another man dressed in black whom he introduced as Reverend Stillwater, a minister. Rose wasn't sure ministers had the same authority as priests, but who was she to question?

"Ready?" Mr. Hardt asked.

She nodded, then slipped a nervous glance at Val who frowned at the floor. He tugged at his coat sleeves, which seemed to fit him just fine. Maybe he was nervous, too.

"All right, then. Step over here next to Mr. Valentine."

Val jerked his head up as if he'd suddenly come out of his troubled musings. He gave her a heart-melting smile and offered his arm.

Mr. Hardt remained near the groom, perhaps to observe or make sure things were done right. Susannah stood at Rose's other side as her attendant. Everyone else took seats on the sofa and in chairs brought in from the dining room.

The minister had a fierce, hawk-like face with pale brown, almost golden, eyes. He had a kind manner, though, and his deep voice rang with a pleasant quality that made it easy to listen to him. He spoke about the sanctity of marriage, read a verse out of his Bible about two joining together to be one, then he launched into the vows.

"Do you, Rose Mary Muldoon, take this man to be your husband; to honor and obey, to care for and serve, in sickness and in health, for richer or poorer, as long as you both shall live?"

"I do." Rose curled her chaffed fingers into the borrowed skirt.

Her groom hadn't acted as if he'd noticed their condition or the too-short skirt or her stockinged toes peeking out from under the frilled petticoats. He'd treated her like the finest lady. She still felt awkward and uncertain. At least she didn't feel *big*. She had to tip her chin to meet his eyes.

His hair, dark as coffee, brushed his coat collar. She longed to smooth the loose strands away from his forehead and run her fingers through it to discover whether it felt as silky as it looked. Just thinking about touching him made her go all warm and shivery.

"Do you, Constantine Jerome..." Reverend Stillwater halted as if he'd forgotten Val's name. "Alexander Valentine..."

With such a highfalutin name, he had to come from some rich family. Why had a man like him chosen a poor girl? Rose shook off the silly daydream. He hadn't *chosen*. She'd offered herself to him, and he only married her to get himself a piece of land. Still, he could've wed any of the women and he had settled for her. A miracle for sure.

"Do you take this woman to be your wife—?"

"I do." Val hadn't waited for the minister to finish the vows.

Reverend Stillwater continued. "And do you promise to protect and provide for her, and to cleave to her in sickness and in health, for so long as you both shall live?"

Val appeared confused by the question. A tense moment passed. Mr. Hardt coughed into his fist.

Rose's face grew warm, then her hands got cold and began to tremble. *Oh no*. Val had changed his mind.

"For as long as possible, I do," he said at last.

Stunned silence followed his pronouncement. He'd changed the vow, somehow made it less binding. Something prevented him from promising a lifetime.

Panic tightened her chest and closed her throat.

Reverend Stillwater's surprise softened to sympathy as his gaze met hers. His eyes seemed to question whether or not to continue. Mr. Hardt scowled but said nothing. A soft sound of distress came from Susannah.

Rose still couldn't speak.

Val clasped her hands. They were so cold and his were so warm. "You have nothing to fear, Rose." He met her eyes without flinching and his voice dropped, whisper-soft. "I swear I will take care of you."

She could only assume whatever prevented a long-term commitment came from some lack on her part, a thought that made the heaviness in her chest worsen. But he'd just promised to care for her. She would trust him to keep his word, and hopefully, she could fix whatever it was he found unacceptable.

She glanced at the minister and with a slight nod permitted him to continue.

The minister brought the Bible to his chest and looked out over the room. "If any man has reason these two should not be wed, let him speak now or forever hold his peace."

Rose held her breath when Mr. Hardt gripped his lapels as if he were about to open his mouth and give a speech. Thank heavens, he didn't. However, he continued to frown at Val as if he disapproved.

"By the power vested in me, I now pronounce you man and wife. What God has joined, let no man put asunder." Reverend Stillwater paused for a heartbeat. "You may kiss the bride."

Val bent his head. Rose's eyelids fluttered shut. As her husband's lips brushed hers, a shower of sparks rained down on her skin—or so it seemed.

She blinked, in a daze, when he straightened, too soon. He could try that kiss again, this time longer.

He slipped an arm around her waist instead.

Reverend Stillwater gave her a nod and shook her husband's hand. "May I be the first to offer my congratulations?"

Susannah embraced Rose, then the rest of the guests rushed forward. The other women hugged her. Some of them cried.

"We've put together some refreshments in the dining room," Mrs. Fry announced.

The owners of the hotel had been so gracious and kind. Everyone had been. The friendly support and encouragement touched a deep, hurting place in Rose's heart. For the first time in months, it felt as if she were part of a family. She'd promised the ladies she would do anything for them, and she meant it.

Val escorted her into the dining room. The table had been pushed up against the wall to make room for people to gather. Mrs. Fry had put out sandwiches and pie, as well as a pitcher of cider. Val fixed a plate for Rose. Before he could get one for himself, Mr. Hardt came up and shook hands. After congratulating Rose, he took her husband aside.

Rose couldn't hear what was said, but Val didn't look pleased.

She put her plate down, unable to eat. Nerves had made her stomach shrink. Mr. Hardt had his chance to object. They were married now. No matter how Val had said the vows, it was a permanent bond in the eyes of God. No one could separate them.

Charm took Rose's elbow and led her away from the table. The petite, golden-haired actress looked exquisite in a soft yellow gown. She looked more like a bride than Rose did. "Don't appear so anxious. He'll think you're easily conquered."

"But I'm his wife. He doesn't need to conquer me."

"Men like a challenge," Charm assured her.

This might be true, but Rose had no experience for a basis to compare, and she wasn't comfortable with pretending or even flirting like other girls. She'd always been awkward and oafish. With Val, she felt more comfortable. And it wasn't just his height. He had a way of putting her at ease, even when she came to him in borrowed clothes with no shoes.

"I'll return your garters tomorrow," Rose promised her friend.

"Keep them...or give them to the next woman who needs them." Charm's eyes shone with affection and wry amusement. "We shall call ourselves the Order of the Garter. And pledge to look out for one another, and to come to each other's aid whenever needed."

"Like sisters."

"Sisters, yes." Charm's face glowed with enthusiasm. "We should have a song, don't you agree? I'll write one."

"Please do."

The talented Miss LaBelle had entertained everyone with songs and poetry during the three-day train ride. She'd talked about performing in Silver City and for gold miners in Montana and being part of a traveling show. Why she'd come to a barren spot in Kansas to marry, she didn't say. But it wouldn't be barren for long by the look of those men who had met the train.

Rose beamed down at her. "Maybe you'll be next."

Charm leaned in and whispered. "I can promise you it won't be anyone Mr. Hardt picks out. Mrs. Braddock and I have agreed to strike."

*Strike?* The word triggered images of women locked out of factories, men put in jail, and rented soldiers firing into a crowd. Rose threw an anxious glance across the room.

Her husband and Mr. Hardt were in deep discussion... about the claim, no doubt. The railroad agent hadn't given an inch, forcing Val to either propose or leave and take his chances. Val had disliked being backed into a corner, and that might account for his hesitancy earlier. But of the two men, he seemed the more reasonable.

"Be careful," Rose warned. "Mr. Hardt's not a bad sort, but he's stubborn, and he likes being in charge."

Charm looked over her shoulder and pursed her lips in disgust. "Yes, he reminds me of another man who thought he could control me. Mr. Hardt won't have any better luck."

"I'm only saying it'll go easier for you if you two don't bash heads."

Her friend's lips turned up and she blinked at Rose innocently. "Who said I'd be the one bashing my head with his?"

Charm drew Rose toward a group of women clustered around Susannah. The widow's knowledge and experience made it natural for her to step into the role of surrogate mother and leader of the group, and she'd shown extraordinary kindness and wisdom.

Except for when it came to Mr. Hardt. His ultimatum, coupled with an abrasive personality, had triggered something fierce and rash inside the genteel widow. Now, it seemed that the slap she'd delivered might not be the last blow. It made Rose fear for her. She'd seen temperamental men take their frustrations out on women.

Rose held back while she considered what she ought to do. Go to her husband's side, which was where she belonged now. The battle between Susannah and Mr. Hardt wasn't her concern. On the other hand, she couldn't walk away from her friends. They were, as Charm had coined, *The Order of the Garter*, bound by friendship and pledged to offer help when needed. She owed it to them to speak to Susannah and urge caution.

It also wouldn't hurt to ask for some advice, considering she knew next to nothing about winning a man's affections.

She cast a yearning glance at her husband and the thudding in her chest grew stronger. By some miracle, she'd gotten the man she wanted. His hesitance to commit must mean he wasn't sure about her. Tonight she had to convince him that he hadn't chosen the wrong girl.

## ❧ 6 ❧

V al delayed retrieving his wife for as long as possible without causing her embarrassment. Not because he didn't wish to be alone with her. That brief kiss had only whetted his appetite for her, and there was the rub.

Bedding his temporary bride would further ensnare her tender heart, not to mention the possibility of giving her a child. Thus far, he'd only descended to the level of a reprobate, not an unconscionable bastard, despite Hardt's accusations. The surly agent planned to distribute women through a raffle. He couldn't legitimately question anyone's motives.

Walking silently across the carpet, Val approached a knot of women gathered around his wife, whispering. It wasn't the hushed giggles of giddy ladies engaged in naughty conversation. Rather, they spoke in low, furtive murmurs that smacked of plots afoot. Rose didn't need to be caught up in the conspiring of unhappy women. She'd be better off with him. For the time being.

His lovely bride glowed with happiness. One of the women had arranged her hair. The reddish-gold color complemented her lightly freckled skin, and she looked positively regal in the borrowed clothing, despite the poor fit.

His gaze moved down her slender neck to the modest collar on the jacket. The sleeves were too short. Otherwise, the outfit enhanced her figure and she seemed delighted to be wearing it. Her petticoat had been lowered to extend the length of her skirts, but it didn't quite cover her tantalizing ankles. The lack of shoes, which would've been the ruination of an English lady, only added to the allure of the lowborn Irish lass. He imagined removing the white stockings and stroking her long, elegant feet.

Desire struck with the force of an unexpected punch and his breath left in a rush. What had happened to his determination to ignore this unfortunate attraction? He jerked his attention to her face, although he'd have to shut his eyes to entirely remove the temptation.

"Rose." His voice came out rough. He hadn't meant to use her familiar name, a breach of manners. It had just popped out. Whenever he looked at her, his head was filled with an image of wild roses, the twining vines heavy with fragrant flowers.

She turned and her eyes widened, wonder rushing into the clear green.

The next blow struck square in the center of his chest. She wouldn't look at him like he'd strewn the stars across the sky after he told her of his plans. But wouldn't it be better if they started with a clear understanding? She'd come out of a destitute situation. She might appreciate what he was willing to do for her.

"Shall we bid adieu to our guests?" He offered her his arm.

She allowed him to tuck her fingers into the crook of his elbow even though she looked a bit confused or perhaps nervous. "We're leaving?"

He couldn't think of a polite way to say he wanted time

with her alone, but no one would question him about retiring with his new bride. "We won't go far. Upstairs."

That remark assured they wouldn't be disturbed. The implication he'd be bedding her also made his wife blush like a... Well, like a rose.

He made a slight bow to five women who'd been standing around her in a protective circle. "Ladies, you all look lovely. Thank you for everything you've done to make this day special. My wife and I shall not forget your kindness. I hope you'll pardon me for taking Rose from you so soon."

The women returned polite smiles. None of the single ladies were debutantes, but he'd expected a few innocent blushes and averted eyes. Instead, they looked him over like they were inspecting him for signs of disease.

"Where will you and Rose stay?" The one who'd posed the question was the spunky widow who'd slapped Hardt after he stupidly offered her up like a prize pig. She was a sharp one and wouldn't be forced to the altar, especially by that rude bore.

Val gave a slight but respectable bow in her direction. "Thank you for your concern. We'll remain here for now. I've rented a bed." He didn't add he wouldn't be sleeping in it.

Mrs. Braddock's sharp gray gaze remained locked on her target. The other women also seemed intent on boring holes through him with their eyes. "You take good care of our Rose, Mr. Valentine. We're all very fond of her."

He could imagine a dozen different ways he could take *good care* of her.

Val cleared his throat, banishing the unproductive image. "Of course. I will treat her as the greatest treasure."

He'd make sure she had a safe place to stay and would settle a tidy sum on her before he left. Rose would be far better off than she had been when she first arrived.

He led her up the stairs. The house-turned-hotel had nice

furnishings in the common rooms. Comfortable, if not elegant. Upstairs, the rooms were sparsely furnished. The floor on the landing wasn't carpeted and no pictures hung on the walls.

Using the key, he opened the door to the room the owners had directed him to take. Folding wooden dividers separated the room into two smaller sleeping quarters, each equipped with a narrow bed, washstand, and chamber pot. Not an ideal arrangement for a newly married couple. Not to mention the beds were made for dwarves.

Val wrestled with disappointment. He hadn't planned on bedding her. Nor would he fool himself into thinking he could crawl under the covers with his tempting wife and remain celibate.

Rose didn't appear surprised by the poor accommodations. Certainly not as annoyed as his former betrothed would've been had he brought her here, although he wouldn't bring Anne to a place like this. But he'd let Rose stay here.

*Thoughtless* wasn't a strong enough word.

She'd hardly uttered a sound since they'd left the dining room.

*Jitters*. His insides danced as well, for a different reason.

"You'll be comfortable here?"

The question elicited a nod.

Nevertheless, he would find her better accommodations before he left town.

Someone had piled up a wad of blankets on the first bed. Open trunks and cases were scattered about on the floor. Val gestured to the divider on the far side of the room. "Our space is over there I presume."

He scooted the screen to make room for them to pass through and noted the same arrangement on the other side, with one addition. "We have a window."

"And a bed..." Rose averted her eyes. "Er, what I mean is, sleepin' in a bed is better than sleepin' on the floor."

If she kept blushing like that, he'd have to remove her clothes so he could see if those blushes colored other areas of her skin.

No! He would keep his hands off her. He would leave the hotel tonight. Then everyone would know they weren't living together as man and wife, and it would embarrass her. But after he'd departed, her unquestionable purity would work in her favor.

The time had come to break the news...gently. He lifted his hands to cup her shoulders then thought better of it and dropped them to his sides. Touching her wouldn't make this news hurt less and would tempt him to do more than just talk.

"Rose, you won't have to stay here for long—"

She spun around to face him with a happy smile. "'Tis a fine place, Val. All that matters is that we're together."

Her simple declaration slipped between his ribs like a well-placed saber thrust. He had to suck in a breath before he could go on.

"We won't."

Her wide eyes searched his. "Won't?"

"Be together." For some awful reason, he couldn't speak in more than two-word sentences.

"Ah. We don't have much time before everyone comes upstairs, you mean?" Her gaze dropped to his mouth and hunger flared in the green depths. "Do you want to...? Will ye please...?" The last three words came out in a whisper. "Kiss me again?"

Every muscle in his body tightened. Primitive signals raced to nerve endings and the blood in his veins thickened and heated. He stared at her parted lips, mesmerized. Her mouth was only a few inches away, so easy to reach. There ought to be a reason he shouldn't, but he couldn't think past the need pounding through him.

Her eyelids lowered to half-mast. He cradled her head at the same time she looped her arms around his middle. He didn't have to draw her to him. Their lips met as if magnetized.

How long they stood there kissing, he didn't know. It could've been a minute or an hour. He'd lost track of time, lost all sense of everything but her sweet taste and her supple body. His hands roved freely over womanly curves and she didn't lift a finger to stop him. Instead, she leaned into him when his fingers shaped her breasts through the jacket bodice.

Her ripeness and eagerness, combined with sweet inno-cence, stoked the fire burning in his loins until it became a roaring blaze. He grew desperate to remove her clothes, layer by layer until he reached her smooth skin and breasts with tips as rosy as her cheeks.

She placed her hand on his jaw and drove her fingers upward, over his ear, threading them through his hair, stroking, tentatively at first, and then with more confidence. Her sighs accompanied his guttural moans as pleasure rippled over his scalp and fanned out across his shoulders and chest. Desire tightened his balls and squeezed until he gasped.

Val fought a mindless urge to bear her to bed, toss her skirts and plunge into her, over and over, until he'd released the inferno.

"Mama?" A child's voice penetrated the sensual haze.

Alarm arrested lust. *Good God.*

Val ripped his lips away, at the same time protectively folding his wife against his pounding heart. He swiveled his head in the direction of the voice.

A boy of perhaps seven or eight peeked around the end of

the divider, the same boy who'd escorted Rose into the parlor before the wedding. Had he followed them up here?

Anger boiled up, joining the stew of uncomfortable emotions, including a heavy spoonful of guilt. Val turned his ire on the intruder. "What are you doing in here, boy?"

"No, don't scare him..." Rose wriggled out of Val's embrace and went immediately to the child. "Danny? Are ye all right, darlin'? Does yer mother know where ye are?"

The child blinked at her, stupefied. His hair stuck up on one side like he'd been sleeping on it. The pile of blankets on the other bed...he must've been beneath them.

Danny rubbed his eyes with a fist. "Got tired."

"I imagine you did, after travelin' so far and all this excitement." Rose ran her fingers through the child's tufted hair, smoothing it into place in a gesture that seemed as natural to her as breathing. "Is that yer stomach makin' that noise? I saw some sandwiches downstairs, and there might be a piece of pie left."

"Pie? I could eat some of that." Danny tugged his coat into place. After throwing a worried look in Val's direction, he raced out the door.

Val's conscience tweaked him. He shouldn't have been so harsh. He should've thanked the lad, not scolded him. If not for his timely intervention, Rose would be unclothed by now, and... And *that* would've ended any hope of giving her a respectable annulment. No matter how tempted, he couldn't act on his urges, not anymore. He'd sworn to control his spontaneous nature and not ruin another person's life.

If he took Rose home with him, his family and those who moved in their circles would shun her. It would be beyond cruel to expose her to that kind of ridicule. Sweet as she was, she could never fit into his life. She'd be better off here, in western America, where people didn't care about bloodlines. His responsibilities awaited him in England. He'd return, possibly win back Anne, if she'd forgive him for jilting her. He still wasn't sure why he'd done it. He'd wanted her for years. But for the life of him, he couldn't bring Anne's image to mind. Not when Rose approached, her face flushed and her lips curved in a welcoming smile.

"Poor Danny. He's not sat down since we got off the train. I'm surprised he woke up. But he's gone now..." In other words, she wanted to take up where they'd left off.

Val reached to straighten his tie. She'd undone the bow. He stared in horror at her gaping bodice. Good God, had *he* done that? Through the thin camisole, he could see the outline of her breasts, pushed up by a tight corset. His mouth became dry as cotton.

She glanced down, appeared surprised, and then covered her mouth, stifling a giggle. "Don't suppose Danny noticed."

Val shook his head, disbelieving. If a beautiful woman had hugged him against her barely covered breasts when he was seven, he would've noticed. "The boy has eyes."

Something in his expression made her smile vanish. She tugged her bodice together and fumbled with the buttons. "I'm sorry. It's not very ladylike..."

No, he would not have her chastise herself for his misbehavior. He caught her hands. "Rose, you did nothing wrong. I'm the one who's to blame for unbuttoning your dress."

The distress on her face faded. "You're me husband, Val. That gives you the right to unbutton anythin' you want..." A smile teased the corners of her mouth. "As long as *I'm* the one wearin' it."

His heart gave a hard twist in his chest. He'd be the lowest cad to take advantage of Rose's sweet vulnerability. He had to extract himself from this marriage before he injured her so badly she would find it impossible to heal. Whatever pain he suffered in the process was no more than he deserved.

He gave her hands a gentle squeeze. "Sweet Rose. I have

no rights where you're concerned. We entered into this marriage quickly. Too quickly. But I promise I'll set things right. As soon as I sell my property, I'll set up a fund for you. Ensure you can be independent, go anywhere you'd like, and marry anyone you want. You'll have something more valuable than a forced marriage. You'll have your freedom."

R ose was struck dumb with astonishment, followed by the sick pitch of her stomach. With just a few words, Val had destroyed her new life. Like the fire that raged through the apartment building where she'd lived, killing the last two people on earth she most loved and who loved her, leaving her without a family or a place to belong. Val had taken everything away and left her with nothing. Nothing she truly wanted.

A tremor started in her chest and moved down her arms to her hands. She withdrew them from his grasp before he felt the shaking. He didn't try to hold on, which just reinforced what he'd told her, that he was ending their marriage. Giving her *freedom*, which sounded more like he was paying her to go away.

"Rose?" The concern on his face didn't match the cruel words that had just fallen from his lips. "You look pale. Sit down before you swoon."

She shook her head. "Tis no swoon I feel. I'm *alamort*."

"*Alamort?*"

He wouldn't know the slang from the world she'd grown

up in. Neither would anyone else, so she'd have to remember to speak regular English.

"Confounded."

She turned and walked past the bed she'd thought they would be sharing, over to the window. The sun blinded her as it fell into the horizon. She felt as if she were falling, too. Falling, her wings on fire, when just a moment ago she'd been soaring. They hadn't been wed for more than two hours and already Val regretted it.

A fearful thought sent her hands to the bodice of the borrowed dress. She touched the buttons to make sure she'd secured them. Val might've been disgusted when she'd paraded her goods in front of Danny. She wasn't a *loose goose*, like he must think. Could be that's why he decided he didn't want her.

The small hairs on her arms and neck prickled, same as what had happened downstairs when he'd come up behind her. Strange, how she'd never been so aware of anyone in her life, and yet he could release her as easy as opening his hand.

"Rose." His low, cultured voice vibrated over her. She hugged her arms, desperate to stop her body's quivering response. How pathetic she must appear, trembling over the sound of her name on his lips.

"I didn't mean to..." he started.

Now he would tell her he'd never wanted her, not even a little bit. Heat scalded her cheeks. "You don't have to apologize. I know you didn't mean to kiss me."

"That's not what I was going to say." His tone held a hint of annoyance. "I meant to kiss you, and I'd be lying if I said I didn't want to kiss you again."

He didn't want her, but he wanted her. He wasn't making any sense, or maybe she was too dull-witted to understand. If he wanted to kiss her again, he had only to touch her, anywhere, and she would turn into his arms.

"What I'm trying to say..." His tone turned soft, regretful. "I never meant to hurt you."

He'd given her hope then ripped it away, and he thought it wouldn't hurt?

Misery clogged her throat. She swallowed so her voice wouldn't come out wobbly and weak. "What did ye think I would feel?"

For a moment, he went silent. He hadn't expected the question, or worse, hadn't even thought about how his indecision might affect her. "There's no excuse, I know. I should've made clear my reasons for entering into marriage."

That wasn't how he'd deceived her.

"Oh, your reasons were clear enough. I knew you was marrying me so you could get Mr. Hardt to sign over that property. I just didn't know you weren't planning on staying married. That's why you wouldn't agree to *as long as you both shall live*."

"I didn't want to lie."

He thought hedging on this detail absolved him.

Anger swept in, giving her a brief respite from her misery and the strength to face him. "You lied when you said *I do*."

His lips tightened and his face muscles froze. Now she knew where the phrase "stiff upper lip" came from. These unfeeling Englishmen. Oh, there might be a flicker of regret in those light-as-crystal eyes, but it could be her mind playing tricks or her foolish, hopeful heart.

She clenched her fists, tempted to strike him, make him bleed like she was bleeding. Only, she'd seen enough violence —in Five Points and with them boys coming home broken from the war—to know it never solved anything. Venting wouldn't change his mind, and afterward, she would only feel worse. If he'd hurt her, wasn't it mostly her fault anyway? She had all but thrown herself at him and he felt pressured into doing something he didn't want to do.

Her shoulders sagged. She relaxed her fists. After losing her family, she survived, and she would do so again after the loss of a husband. One she'd known only a few hours.

Sinking onto the side of the bed, she leaned forward and put her head in her hands.

Val sat beside her.

He was a strange one. Hadn't he just said he was done with her? Yet, here he remained, hovering like a worried uncle.

She cocked her head and stole a furtive look out of the side of her eyes. He'd propped his arms on his knees and stared at the floor. Did he have mixed feelings or was he just hesitant to go downstairs and draw questioning looks? He might be worried he wouldn't get his deed signed.

A cool breeze from the open window bathed her heated skin. The setting sun had turned the sky brilliant shades of red and orange. If she weren't so miserable, she would get up and look, having never seen sunsets like these. Soon, it would be evening. People would think they were up here doing what freshly married folks generally do, what her body ached for. He'd awoken something inside her with his kiss, and his continued presence tormented her.

"What are you sitting here for? I thought you said I was a mistake."

He straightened, gripped her by her arm to pull her to face him, and took hold of her shoulders. "You are not a mistake. That is not how I think of you, not at all. You're a very lovely, appealing woman. If my situation were different..."

What was he saying? There might be a chance she could fix it for him.

"What situation?"

His grip on her shoulders softened and he let his hands trail down her arms before he removed them altogether, seemingly with reluctance. "The reason I'm here, the only reason I came to America is to make my fortune. So I can...I have to restore... What I've been trying to say is, I'm not staying, Rose. I must return home."

She let his explanation sink in, what he'd said without actually saying it. A poor Irish girl wasn't part of his plans. Why should she be? The way he spoke, his manner, and his clothing, all indicated an upbringing far above hers. She'd known that the moment he'd opened his mouth. Had they happened to meet in New York, which wouldn't have been likely, he'd have paid her no notice. A high bloke like him would've been far beyond her reach. But out here, where stars twinkled so bright that they looked close enough to touch, she had reached for one and caught it. She should've known she couldn't keep him.

Or could she?

She studied his profile, lingering on his firm lips. He'd said he wanted her, the way he kissed her and touched her confirmed it, and he'd called her *lovely* and *appealing*. That didn't sound like a man who wanted to get rid of her. If she learned to be a lady, he might reconsider.

Without education, with limited resources, how could she learn enough to be the kind of wife he'd be proud to have by his side?

Susannah could help. She displayed a well-bred upbringing, perhaps not as lofty as Val's, but good enough that she'd know the finer points of being a lady. In return, Rose could offer to watch Danny while Susannah held court to find a proper suitor.

Rose relaxed her fingers from their tight grip together and her despair eased somewhat. She might have a chance if granted a little more time. "When will you leave for England?"

He cocked his eyebrow at her. Was he surprised she

hadn't fallen into weeping or begging? She was stronger than that. Maybe fine ladies blubbered and carried on. She'd have to ask Susannah about it.

"Are you ready to be rid of me?" he asked softly. "I wouldn't blame you."

She shook her head emphatically. "Oh no, you can't leave until you get your fortune."

Val's lips formed a wry smile. "We'll have to wait to see if it can be called that. First, I have to take a look at the property, and do some drilling to see if the rumor is true about coal deposits. Then I'll need to do a survey."

Rose breathed easier. "That'll take some time. We had better stay married until you get it sorted out so nobody can challenge your claim."

"You'd be willing to do that?" He sounded astonished that she'd gone along with what he'd mapped out before his conscience had chided him to come clean. "You'd remain my wife? Even though you know it can't be...it won't be for long?"

Her confidence wavered. It would take a miracle. Then again, it *had* been a miracle when he'd been the first man to walk through the door of the hotel. She'd taken it as a sign from God, and she must hold tight to that belief.

Rose shifted on the bed to face him and converse more easily. She just wanted to be able to look at him. He was so pleasing to the eye.

"Ye said..." First off, she had to stop sounding so Irish. "You want to help me, so it's only fair I help you. I don't think you should say anything to anybody about leaving just yet. We'll go on like everything's fine, and then when the time comes, you just leave. Make up a story about somebody dying, and then just don't come back."

The surprise on his face would have been amusing if she'd felt like laughing. "Are you certain? You're willing to pretend we're happily married for the time it takes to get this thing settled?"

If things went the way she hoped, he'd be taking her with him. Not that she had much interest in moving to England. She'd prefer to stay here and make a home somewhere she felt she could easily fit in. But he wasn't having it, and she wasn't willing to let him go to look for another husband. This one suited her better than any man she'd ever met.

"I am. If you're willing to pretend along with me."

## ❧ 8 ❧

The next morning, Val escorted Rose to breakfast in the dining room. She wanted to sit near her friends, and she put on a perfect act, playing the part of the blushing bride on the day after her wedding. No one would guess her husband had slept on the floor.

Sleep was too generous a word. He'd spent the night wide awake thinking about his wife who lay just a few feet away. For some reason, knowing they were wed stimulated his lust like nothing else. After he'd told her of his plans, Rose had done nothing to beguile him, other than being beautiful and sweet. He didn't know how he'd manage another night without touching her.

Not only had erotic thoughts robbed his rest, but guilt had also done its part as well. Every time he closed his eyes, he saw the stricken look on Rose's face when he'd told her they wouldn't remain married. He hadn't thought it possible to hate himself more than he already did.

Her response flummoxed him. No tears or recriminations, which he'd expected. Instead, after a few tense moments, she'd seemed to accept it and even suggested they act as if nothing were amiss because it would make things go smoother. Perhaps she'd decided he wasn't worth as much as the money she stood to gain from the sale of the property. An unflattering thought.

The truth hurt, didn't it?

Val finished the fluffy American biscuit without really enjoying it and drank down a cup of coffee laced with sugar and cream, trying to eat fast without appearing to rush. The sooner he settled his claim and sold the land, the sooner he could depart, which would be the best thing for both of them.

He laid his napkin on the table, stood, and sketched a slight bow. "I'll leave you ladies to enjoy the morning."

Rose glanced up at him and her porcelain skin turned pink. How did she do that? He'd never seen anyone fake blushing. Perhaps it wasn't false. "Where are you off to?"

She could be embarrassed or worried someone might find out they were pretending. He'd better get going before he gave away their secret.

"Mr. Hardt will have the paperwork ready. After I meet with him, I'll be going out to take a look at the property. Don't expect I'll return before dinner."

Something hopeful and heartbreaking filled her eyes. "Would you take me along? I'd like to see it. The property, that is."

He had no idea what he'd find or who, and he refused to expose Rose to danger. Not to mention the temptation of being alone with her. He had less impulse control than most, and he didn't want to test it with his temporary wife. "After I see what we're dealing with."

Leaning down, he gave her a quick kiss on the cheek. The twin stains on her cheeks deepened from pink to red, triggering a hot rush of blood somewhere much lower than his face. He turned on his heel and left before anyone noticed he was growing hard as a stone.

The morning air had a clean, crisp quality. It smelled of grass and something elemental, earthy, not quite like the countryside at home, but much nicer than the air in London where he'd frittered away much of his time—and his inheritance.

His father had purchased him a one-way passage to America. A telling gesture. When he returned with his coffers replenished and his debts repaid, he might be acquitted of his crime of being a *disappointment*. Nevertheless, he'd still need to marry a woman who had a title and estate, as he had neither. For once, he would remain focused on the goal, even if it didn't excite him as much as it had before he'd wed Rose.

Sweet Rose. He couldn't let himself become attached. A poor Irish lass could never fit in with his family. She would feel more rejected and outcast than he'd felt over most of his life, for different reasons. Here, she could find a husband who could give her the kind of life and love she deserved.

It was a fairly short walk to the land office, but Val couldn't make his feet move fast. Hardt had given him a lecture about hedging his vows, saying Rose deserved better. That, Val couldn't dispute. Nevertheless, he wouldn't give Hardt another chance to chastise him. He'd get right to the point and keep the discussion related to business.

Unlike the shabby structures housing the saloons and few other businesses, the land office was a neat frame building like one might find back east. Given the scarcity of lumber, it had probably been shipped in, ready to assemble. In America, anything could be ordered from a catalog—stores, schools, churches, even brides—and trains would bring it. Fueled by coal.

Armed with the assurance of making a fortune, Val opened the door.

Hardt sat behind a desk strewn with papers. He'd shed his coat, apparently comfortable doing business in his vest and rolled-up shirtsleeves, another Western peculiarity.

The office took up a single room with filing cabinets in the back and bookcases pushed up against another wall. Behind the desk, large maps showing completed and projected railway routes across the region.

Until Val closed the door, he didn't see the men seated to his right: Jarvis, looking every bit the sore loser, and O'Shea. The Irish saloonkeeper offered a sympathetic smile.

The man behind the desk stood. "Mr. Valentine, good morning. I thought we'd see you soon. I told Mr. Jarvis and Mr. O'Shea to wait." Hardt gestured to a chair close to the desk. "Have a seat."

Alarms sounded in Val's head. He considered the possible reasons the railroad agent would've invited these two men to join them and could come up with nothing good. He held onto his hat brim and remained standing which gave him a natural height advantage, as well as the ability to get away if for some reason the three decided to gang up on him. After a few run-ins with surly miners who'd lost at cards, he'd learned to plan for quick exits.

"Thank you, but I can't afford a delay. I am here to pick up the assigned deed." He trained his attention on the land agent while keeping the other two men in his peripheral vision. "I assume everything is in order."

"Hell no, it ain't in order, you uppity bastard." Jarvis shot to his feet. His sparse mustache twitched like whiskers and his black, beady eyes filled with malice.

Rats didn't frighten Val, but rabid ones could be dangerous.

O'Shea leaned back in his seat and crossed his ankle over his knee as if preparing to watch a show. Val didn't intend to give him one.

"The assigned deed?" he said in a clipped voice. "May I have it?"

Hardt didn't touch any of the numerous documents scattered in front of him. "Mr. Jarvis has challenged your right to his claim."

"Knew you'd see it my way, Mr. Hardt," Jarvis said with a smirk. He gripped the lapels of his loose-fitting coat and shook loose a shower of dirt. He not only looked like a rat—he was as filthy as one. "That cheatin' gambler's tryin' to steal my property."

Val maintained his hold on his hat brim and his temper. Snatching the rodent by his lapels and heaving him through the glass window might feel good, but it wouldn't result in getting his claim validated. He had never cheated at cards. His sharp memory, observation skills, and instincts helped him win--often. Impulsiveness had been his downfall, not dishonesty.

"The whining excuse of every sore loser I've ever met," Val replied in an unconcerned tone.

He gave the land agent a questioning look, wondering at the man's next move.

Hardt addressed the Irishman. "Mr. O'Shea, did you observe the game? Did Mr. Valentine cheat?"

Val's chest tightened. He'd been set up, just as he thought.

O'Shea didn't blink. "Jarvis bet his deed. He put down a losing hand. That's pretty much the way it looked to me."

Jarvis dropped his jaw, then he turned on O'Shea with his hands fisted. "What the hell, you stupid Mick! You know damn well he cheated. There ain't no other way he could've won that many times."

Val blinked in astonishment as the Irishman unfolded out of his chair. His smile turned brittle. "We don't allow cheating at O'Shea's. A warning's posted on a sign. Them that don't abide by the rule are taken outside and shot. None of the others at the table felt the need to shoot Mr. Valentine, and they'd emptied their pockets, too."

"Then it's settled."

Jarvis whipped around at Hardt's statement, which had been delivered with the tone of an ultimatum, and his face darkened to the color of a beet. "No! Nothing's settled!"

He advanced on Hardt, fists raised and shouting. Before Val could intercept him, Hardt reached beneath the desk and withdrew a large revolver. He didn't point it or even cock it, but he had a deadly glint in his eyes. "Mr. Jarvis, I suggest you take your leave. Now."

Jarvis halted in his tracks. "But...that's *my* land."

Hardt's flat expression didn't shift. "It *was* your land. You gambled it away."

"You-you can't do this. I-I'll..." Jarvis trembled with rage.

"You're welcome to discuss your case with a lawyer or with the judge when he's in town. In the meantime, under the authority of the railroad, I'm assigning the land to Mr. Valentine. If you make trouble, Lieutenant Goldman will escort you out of town. If you wish to stay in the area, I suggest you go find another claim to improve. Good day, Mr. Jarvis."

A fine speech, and delivered with less emotion than if he'd been discussing the weather.

Jarvis crushed his hat in his hand. With a final glare at Val, he turned and stormed out, slamming the door behind him.

Val stared after the loser in amazement. He hadn't expected this turn of events. It was possible he'd fallen asleep on that hard floor and was having a strange dream.

O'Shea settled a black felt hat on his head and smoothed the brim with his fingers as he spoke. "Well, then. I'm off. Got work to do. You know where to find me if you need anything more." He said this to Hardt, and then he offered Val his hand. "Watch yer back."

Val returned the Irishman's beefy grip. "I will. Thank you for vouching for me."

"Didn't do it for you. Can't have folks thinkin' I allow cheatin' in my place. Wouldn't be good for business." As he left, he tossed a remark over his shoulder. "If any of them women happen to be looking for work instead of a husband, send her my way."

The comment baffled Val. The Irishman had to be the only man in town who didn't want a wife. Perhaps whatever injury had given him a slight limp had damaged him in a worse way. Awful to think about.

Hardt slipped the gun back into a desk drawer. He might consider carrying one if he made a habit of collecting enemies like that rat, Jarvis.

"Did you ask those two to come here to dispute my claim?" Val asked. Utter fatigue had set in, which had to be the reason for the fog in his brain that prevented him from deciphering Hardt's motive.

Hardt glanced up with an expression of mild surprise. "No. I asked them to meet us here so we could resolve a dispute without violence. If I assigned the land to you without establishing ownership in front of a reliable witness, Jarvis could make trouble for both of us."

Val's stomach pitched. He'd seen the results of vigilante justice dangling from the thick branch of a tree.

Hardt was right. Jarvis would appeal to the other settlers in his quest for revenge. But O'Shea had popularity and trust, and he'd be telling a different story in his saloon where so many men gathered and gossiped. Jarvis would be pegged as a sore loser and would have a hard time recruiting supporters. It showed smart thinking on the part of the railroad agent, considering the poor judgment he'd shown yesterday.

"That's downright decent of you. I owe you a debt," Val readily admitted, offering his hand. "Thank you."

Hardt didn't return the handshake. "You don't owe me anything. I'm tasked with doing whatever is necessary to settle disputes and keep construction moving."

He picked up an envelope and handed it over the desk to Val with a cold eye. "I've assigned you the land. But the only reason I did is that I'm honor-bound to do so, given you've met the stipulations decreed by the railroad. I personally think you are lower than a rattlesnake for tricking Miss Muldoon into thinking you'll stick around. I know your type. You'll be out of here as soon as you pocket the proceeds from the sale."

Val took the envelope. He'd not offer his hand again, not to a man who held him in such contempt. The cut stung worse for having more than a grain of truth. "Regardless of what you think, I would never leave Rose without resources."

"By that, you mean you offered her money? Did you consider asking her first if money was what she wanted?"

Money was what every woman wanted.

Only, Rose hadn't turned out to be like every other woman.

Val refused to be dragged into another argument. His conscience had been flaying him for the past eighteen hours. He was well aware he'd taken advantage of Rose's attraction to him, but she seemed to have gotten over him. Enough to play along.

He put on his hat and tucked the envelope into his pocket. Whatever he made, he would give her half. It was the least he could do, as well as seeing to it that she had a nice place to stay and dresses that covered her ankles. "I will take care of my wife."

Hardt held his gaze, unrelenting. "And who will take care of her after you're gone?"

There was something about the railroad agent's fierce defense that seemed stronger than the usual concern a gentleman showed for a lady. Hardt had a tender spot for Rose. The way his expression softened whenever he looked at her confirmed it, as well as the possibility he would step in to fill the void.

Jealousy blistered Val's heart. "Are you implying you'll be the one taking care of her?"

The contempt in Hardt's gaze turned to disgust. "Only a foul mind could come up with something so base. In case you hadn't noticed, your *wife* is barely an adult. I'd wager she hasn't seen twenty summers."

The land agent reached over the desk, took a pen out of its holder, dipped it into an inkwell, and went back to writing whatever he'd been working on earlier. His actions made it clear he'd ended the conversation.

Val left the office simmering. Hardt's rudeness grated on him, but it wasn't nearly as vexing as the man's interest in Rose. Granted, she deserved to find a good husband, but the stodgy railroad agent wasn't right for her. Not at all. Stunted personality. Humorless. Dour.

Rose had remarkable optimism, given her impoverished background, and an appealing playfulness that needed to be encouraged. Hardt would stifle her. He was right about one thing, though. Rose was young and innocent. As such, she deserved to be awakened with tenderness and sensitivity, shown all the ways in which she was beautiful and desirable, coaxed into blooming like the flower she was named after.

Val decided he would do something else for Rose before he left.

He would find her the right man.

## 9

A fter breakfast, Rose followed Susannah into the parlor. She had to get her friend to help her learn how to be a lady as soon as possible. There was no time to waste.

Val had gulped down his food and rushed out the door in a big hurry to get to the railroad office and escape her. He didn't have to say it. She knew. Last night, she'd heard the floorboards creak as he'd moved restlessly, heaving repeated sighs of frustration. At dawn, he'd slipped out, quietly, so as not to wake anyone. He needn't have worried about her. She wasn't asleep and hadn't been for most of the night.

In the parlor, Susannah settled into a wingback chair. She took her time, adjusting her skirts while her son, Danny, hopped onto a matching chair positioned on the other side of a marble-topped table.

Rose hesitated. She wanted to be close enough to talk to Susannah, but she'd have to pull up a chair, and then she might be a bother if her friend had other plans for the morning.

"Danny, you need to work on your penmanship."

Susannah reached into a satchel and withdrew a writing slate and a piece of chalk.

Her son made a face. "Do I hafta?"

"*Must I?*"

Danny huffed and drooped over the slate in his lap. He did a fine job of putting on a miserable expression. "*Must I* sit here? I saw some kids outside earlier. They were playing."

"School before play."

How would Susannah find a suitor if she was busy with her son?

Rose thought of something that might help all three of them if Susannah would agree.

"I'll sit beside ye," she offered. "Will you show me your writing?"

This seemed to perk him up and Susannah's relieved expression gave Rose extra hope. She moved a chair next to him and sat down.

"Can you do your alphabet?" She was proud to have learned as much as she had, which included knowing her letters and numbers. Her Da had taught her how to add and subtract so she wouldn't get cheated. She knew enough schooling to get by, but not nearly enough about acting like a lady to impress her husband.

"Shoot, that's easy. I can do more than the alphabet." Danny bent over the slate and began to write a word. The chalk screeched, sending shivers over Rose's arms. Danny glanced up with an apology in his eyes. "Sorry. That happens when I press down too hard."

"Makes me shiver. That means you're doing a good job."

"Really?" He beamed at her with obvious pride.

She smiled and couldn't resist ruffling his hair, as she'd done so often with Willy. "You'll be smarter than those chuckleheads outside. Then they'll wish they had a mother who could teach them."

"Chuckleheads?" Smiling, he bent over the slate. "How do I spell that?"

Rose gasped. Name-calling wasn't what Susannah would want to be teaching him. "Spell this instead: *silly Rose*."

Susannah's soft release of breath sounded like a laugh, but Rose glanced up to be sure. Sure enough, her friend's eyes shone with amusement. "I don't think I've ever seen him so interested in penmanship. Thank you, Rose."

"You're welcome. I'm happy to help out with Danny as much as I can. I used to watch over my little brother Willy..." Rose stopped mid-sentence. That wasn't what she'd come in here to talk about, her losses. With Susannah's help, she'd not have to bear another loss, made worse by rejection. "Would you help me learn to be a lady?"

Susannah's eyebrows shot upward.

Danny snickered.

Rose felt her face grow warm. She wondered if they both thought the task would be impossible.

"Miss Rose, you *are* a lady." Danny giggled through his nose and pointed somewhere in the vicinity of her chest. He'd interpreted her words literally, like most children.

Playing along, she looked down at herself and made a surprised face. "Why, you're right! I hadn't noticed."

Danny doubled over with laughter.

Rose turned to plead with Susannah who wouldn't have misinterpreted what she said. "Please, I could repay you for your help. I'll wash for you, watch Danny when you need to go out."

Susannah lifted her hand. "Rose, I don't need payment. I'd be happy to teach you anything within my scope of knowledge. But Danny is right. You are a lady. In the truest sense of the word."

Rose shook her head. "No, I'm not. Not the right sort of lady." She searched for the words. "The kind of lady I need to be is the type Val would have on his arm if he hadn't been pushed into marrying me."

"If anyone has been *pushed*, it's you." Susannah clutched her hands in her lap and her eyes turned darker, the color of a storm cloud about to erupt. "Mr. Hardt knew better, he's just so...so..."

"Hard-headed." Rose supplied a nicer word than what her friend might come up with. The two were matched in stubbornness, but she didn't point that out. "And I wasn't pushed. I as much as asked him to marry me, so if anyone was doing the pushing, it was me."

Susannah stood abruptly. "I believe I hear someone calling us. Danny, continue to work on your penmanship. Rose and I will be back in a moment."

Before Rose could react, her friend motioned her to follow.

When they reached the front hallway, Susannah led her to the door and outside to the porch. Once they were beyond her son's hearing, she whirled around and clasped hands. "Rose, Mr. Valentine took advantage of you and your interest in him. You don't have to prove anything to that opportunist."

Rose fought a downward tug on her confidence which had been doing pretty well after Val had kissed her and declared he wanted to do it again. "You don't think he likes me?"

The intensity on Susannah's face softened. She gave a gentle squeeze before she released her hands. "I've seen the way he looks at you, Rose. He likes you. More than likes you. Why do you believe you need to impress him? Is it because of something he said? Or did?"

Rose looked down, too embarrassed to say her husband hadn't *done* anything. She pressed her hand against her stomach to still the anxious fluttering. It wouldn't be right to share those confidences after she'd told Val she would keep quiet about their agreement. "I just want to make him proud to have me on his arm. That's all."

Susannah opened her mouth as if she might say something else, but then she closed it. "All right, I'll help you impress your Mr. Valentine."

Before Rose could speak her thanks, a handful of her skirt was in Susannah's fist.

"First, we must get rid of this and purchase you some proper unmentionables. And shoes."

Susannah had helped her dress for the wedding. She'd seen the patched undergarments and had loaned the corset and bustle. Rose didn't much like the corset, but it had proved useful in holding things in and up. Not to mention, proper ladies wore them.

Rose drew her shawl closed to cover the ugly dress. Inside the boots, she curled her toes to prevent them from protruding through her worn woolen stockings. "I got no balsam."

"Balsam?"

"Money." Rose wrung her hands. She'd never get this *lady* business right; she couldn't even talk properly. "Sorry, got to remember not to use slang."

"Dear Rose, it's your husband's *responsibility* to clothe you. That's what a gentleman does." Susannah released her hold on the dress and smiled at Rose. "Give me an hour with Danny. Afterward we'll go see what we can find at the mercantile, and we'll put it on your husband's credit."

Rose shook her head. Val hadn't offered to purchase new clothes for her. He might expect her to buy them with the money he planned to give her. "I'm not so sure."

Susannah raised a finger and waggled it at her. "No arguments. You said you wanted to look and act like a lady. Consider this your first lesson."

An hour later Rose clomped along behind Susannah and

Danny, trying her best to mimic the way her friend's hips swayed beneath the bustled skirt. The slight swing looked natural for Susannah. Rose felt like a long-legged colt wearing big, clumsy boots.

Susannah said they would first look for an everyday walking dress, such as the one she'd donned, light gray wool with black velvet trim. It wasn't a color Rose would pick, but it complimented Susannah's ash-blond hair and made her gray eyes look lighter. She knew how to dress to bring out the best in her shape and coloring.

Rose made a mental note to ask about what colors and styles would look best on her. Ladies knew such things. Those from families like Val's might be born with fashion sense for all she knew. This business of learning to be a lady was going to take some time. Only, she didn't have time. She had to hurry up and learn as fast as she could, and then she might stand a chance of convincing Val to keep her.

Susannah halted at the corner where two muddy streets intersected. She kept her hand on Danny's shoulder as they waited for a wagon to creak past. The man driving it nearly twisted his neck off to look at her. She acted like she hadn't noticed, but it was impossible to miss.

What kind of man would interest a lady like Susannah? For some reason, Mr. Hardt's scowling face popped into Rose's head. She laughed out loud.

Susannah turned at the sound. "What do you find so funny?"

"Oh, nothing." Rose swallowed her laughter. She'd never convince Susannah to consider Mr. Hardt as a candidate, but there had to be another strong man out there who'd suit her.

Susannah made her way across the unpaved street with careful steps, but there was no way she could prevent her spool heels from sinking into the mud.

At times, flat-soled boots came in handy, whether or not they were ladylike.

Two men stood on the corner, ogling them as they crossed the street. The thin one wore his denim trousers held up with straps and had a holstered pistol on a belt.

Rose wasn't used to seeing so many men wearing guns, but out here, everyone seemed to have them. She couldn't recall whether Val wore one, but to her way of thinking, it spoke well of him if he didn't. Men who carried guns were more apt to resort to violence to resolve disputes.

The taller man's coat sleeves strained against bulging muscles in his shoulders and arms. He didn't wear a gun. Not one she could see.

As Susannah approached, the brawny man lifted his hat. "Mornin' ma'am."

"Good morning." Susannah smiled and continued into the store.

The cove with shifty eyes clipped Danny on the shoulder. "You takin' good care of your mama, short stuff?"

"Yes sir," he replied politely and ducked the man's second attempt to clap him on the back. Rose moved up behind Danny before the man could try again.

He looked up at her and his jaw dropped. "Good golly, you're a long drink of water."

Rose gave him no reaction. It was best to ignore this kind of rudeness, something she had put up with ever since she'd reached her full height at sixteen.

"Don't mind Ned," drawled the man behind her. "He ain't seen ladies in so long, he's plum forgot his manners." The soft-spoken one wasn't quite her height, but the breadth of his shoulders blocked her view of the street.

"Top o' the morning to you, miss. Arch Childers, at your service." He swept off his black hat, releasing long, shaggy hair, and made an exaggerated bow. When he straightened, his eyes twinkled with merriment. "That's how you greet a lady, Ned. You don't tell her she's a long drink of water."

Rose returned his friendly smile. This Mr. Childers had some rough edges, but he wasn't a bad article to look at, and he seemed friendly and considerate. Susannah might be able to bring him up to her standards given a little time. The thought barely had time to form before she reappeared and grabbed Rose's arm.

"Excuse us. We're in a bit of a hurry." Susannah didn't give Rose a chance to introduce her to Mr. Childers before she pulled her into the store.

"Maybe you should meet the man outside—"

"I saw him. He was rude to you and he bothered Danny."

"No, not that one..." Rose smelled smoke. Not burning wood. Meat? She jerked to a stop in front of a blackened haunch dangling from the ceiling beams. Pots and pans were displayed similarly. She had better watch her head.

"Candy!" Danny raced past his mother.

A bearded man behind the counter lifted a peppermint stick out of a jar and handed it to the excited child. "Here you go, son."

Susannah caught up and restrained Danny before he could accept the treat. "No, thank you, sir. We don't need candy."

Danny's face fell. "Mama, please! I haven't had any in so long."

The shopkeeper's smile turned sympathetic and he extended the candy again. "Let the boy have it. My treat."

"That's very kind." Susannah turned to her son. "What do you say?"

"Thank you, mister," Danny spoke around the candy stick he'd put into his mouth. He gazed up at his mother questioningly. "Can I look 'round?"

"If you promise not to touch anything."

"I p'womise." He wandered toward the back, making loud sucking sounds.

"Stay where I can see you," Susannah called after him.

"We can hear him," Rose assured her.

The shopkeeper came around the counter toward Susannah. He smoothed his beard then rolled down his shirt sleeves and dusted off an apron that wasn't dirty. "I'm George Appleton, the owner of this store. You ladies must've arrived on the bride train."

Susannah acted oblivious to his preening. "The bride train?"

"That's what we call it when the railroad brings out a load of brides. Girard got their brides in March. It's about time we got ours."

The slight widening of Susannah's eyes told Rose she'd finally become aware of this man's interest. She moved back a step.

Rose found her friend's reaction curious. The shopkeeper wasn't bad looking, he didn't smell, and he'd been nice to Danny

"We are looking for readymade women's clothing," Susannah told him. "Would you have anything?"

"Just got in a shipment. Ordered them special for you ladies." Mr. Appleton sent her a hopeful smile.

*Poor man.* Susannah wasn't even looking at him. She'd sailed off in the direction of the dresses, still talking. "We need a proper traveling suit that will fit my friend, along with some other things."

The "other things" would be what Susannah called *unmentionables*.

Rose held her smile while the shopkeeper slowly appraised her. The distress wrinkling his forehead told her they were wasting their time. "Never mind, I don't need readymade. Just show me the fabrics and I'll make me own."

Relief flooded Mr. Appleton's face. "Fabrics. Yes! The bolts of fabric are in the back. I'll show you."

After he set out for the rear of the store, Susannah whirled around. "We can make a dress later. Let's just buy one now."

"None of 'em will fit," Rose explained.

Susannah's blank expression showed she hadn't thought it through. "Oh." She turned back to the shelf stacked with folded dresses. "If we find something you like, I can help you add to the length. I'm a good seamstress."

While Susannah sorted through the readymade clothes, Rose went to look at fabric. The shopkeeper showed her the table and then went off to make another attempt at getting Susannah's attention. He was persistent, but she'd given him no encouragement.

Out of the side of her eye, Rose noticed the two men she'd seen earlier enter the store. They made their way to the back, conversing as they walked. She pretended not to notice them and turned her attention to the bolts of fabric.

As they drew closer, their low conversation drifted over.

"That gambler stole my claim, and Hardt let him! They ain't gonna get away with it."

"You lost your land playing poker, Ned. You oughta know when to stop betting."

"What's this Arch? You on his side?"

"On my own side, which right now means stayin' outta trouble. I got bigger things to worry about than fixin' problems that wouldn't be problems if you showed a lick of sense."

"If you won't help, then I'll take care of it myself." The man named Ned growled his threat and then stalked out of the store.

The gambler he'd mentioned had to be Val.

Rose put her hand to her chest where her heart beat so hard she could feel it. That *gnarler* might just be barking, but how could she be sure? After all, he wore a gun. She had to find her husband and warn him.

She whirled around and nearly collided with Mr. Childers.

He flashed a bright smile. "Hey there, Miss. I didn't get your name."

"You ought to be ashamed of yourself," Rose shot back, passing him before he could respond. He might not be encouraging that other man, but he hadn't done anything to stop him either, which put Arch Childers in the category of *enemy*, as far as she was concerned.

Susannah had several dresses spread out on a table, doing her best to ignore the hovering shopkeeper without appearing rude. Danny had found a sack of marbles and had crawled under the table to play with them.

Rose knew she had to come up with a good excuse for leaving the store without them. They didn't need to be involved in something that could turn dangerous. She slowed her pace to casual and put on a hapless smile. "Marriage must make women forgetful. I just now remembered I told Val that I'd meet him at Mr. Hardt's office. If you don't mind, I'll pop over there for a minute. Meet you at the hotel."

Susannah's brow creased like she was debating whether to offer to go along. But she wouldn't. After slapping Mr. Hardt yesterday, she'd avoided the land agent like he had the itch. "Wouldn't you like to look at these dresses first?"

Rose couldn't waste another second. That man might be on his way to find Val and shoot him. "Ah, no, I'm no good at this. Just pick something you like. I'm sure it'll be fine."

"But you wanted to learn."

"I will. Soon as I get back, I'll put me mind to me studies."

"It's *my*...my studies."

"' Course it is." Rose gave a wave over her shoulder as she flew out the door.

The man who'd threatened Val was nowhere in sight. Had he gone to the railroad office? Sounded like he'd been there and might've even seen Val.

She lifted her skirts and ran, her mind filled with awful premonitions. Her husband sprawled on the floor in a spreading pool of blood, his eyes staring upward, sightless. Smoke from the gun, and the killer's cackling laugh. Loose planks shuddered beneath her feet, jarring her knotted insides.

*Merciful Mary, please. Don't let anything bad happen to him.*

## 10

Still smarting over his earlier encounter with the land agent, Val headed to O'Shea's to plant the seeds for a plan to find his replacement. Hardt was most definitely off the list. The Irish saloon owner had shown courage by telling the truth and standing up to Jarvis. He was worth checking out.

Inside the busy saloon, the proprietor was at his usual post, serving drinks and wiping down his spotless bar. His establishment wasn't fancy by any stretch, but it appeared well-kept and clean, as did the man who owned it. The same couldn't be said for his customers.

Val rested his arm on the bar and nodded when O'Shea lifted a bottle of expensive whiskey. He had to continue the appearance of having wealth. If the locals found out about his desperate situation, potential buyers wouldn't offer him top dollar for his land.

He turned slightly to keep an eye on the door in case Jarvis showed up. Whether the sore loser would act on his threats was hard to say. Best to be prepared, and keep Rose safely tucked away with her new friends.

O'Shea set a glass on the counter and poured. "What are you doing here? Aren't you just married?"

"Yesterday." Val slid a coin across the bar. He would pay his debts—all of them—and that included the one he owed to Rose. "My lovely wife is with her friends this morning. I would like nothing better than to while away the time in her company, but we have come to an understanding about the temporal nature of our matrimonial situation."

The barkeeper's uncomprehending stare reminded Val that he shouldn't assume everyone in the room could read or write...or understand his language.

"We were married for the sake of convenience. Once I've established the value of the land I own, I will sell out and move on. Rose will not be leaving with me."

"She refused to go?" O'Shea's tone conveyed disbelief.

No woman alive would remain in this squalor if a husband offered her a way out, and Val wouldn't impugn Rose. "I can't take her home."

Understanding dawned on O'Shea's broad face, along with another expression that was just as easy to read. Disgust. "You *won't* take her, is what you meant. She's not high enough in her instep for your kind."

The insults struck their target. Val's conscience. He couldn't dispute O'Shea's blunt assessment of his decision to leave Rose behind, even if her impoverished background wasn't the only reason.

Rose needed a husband she could rely on. A man who was even-tempered, gentle, steady and dependable. All the things he wasn't. Mostly, she deserved a man who could commit his whole heart to her, not just one who lusted after her and was willing to use her. Most of all, this was reason enough to let her go. He didn't deserve a woman as sweet and guileless as the one he'd married.

"I intend to give her half the proceeds from the sale." He

patted his hand over the coat pocket where the deed pressed against his chest. What should've produced a reassuring feeling instead curdled into guilt and self-loathing.

He'd feel differently when he made Rose an independent woman. "She'll be able to pick the husband she wants rather than have one thrust upon her," he explained to O'Shea.

The brawny Irishman folded his arms across his chest. "What makes you think she hasn't already done that?"

The knot in Val's chest dropped like a stone through his stomach. The image of Rose's adoring gaze came back to haunt him, as did her crushed expression when he'd told her of his plans. "She's young and healthy and experiencing attraction. Her fascination with me will pass when she meets a man who is better suited to her. I wager she'll forget all about me within less than a fortnight after she marries again."

Why did he find that idea repugnant?

O'Shea's frown gathered over the storm in his eyes. "You'll take the honey and then pass the pot to some other man. Is that how it is?"

Val curled his fist at the insult. He owed this uppity fellow no explanation. However, he might have to offer one if he hoped to gain O'Shea's agreement to court Rose. "She will remain chaste. After I've sold the land and put half of the proceeds in her name, we will apply for an annulment. I will take full responsibility."

"That's big of you." O'Shea's snide tone reinforced his low opinion.

Instead of giving in to anger, Val conceded the truth to himself and then responded with a challenge. "Look around. Identify the men in this room who are marrying for purposes outside of greed and self-gratification."

The Irishman's gaze remained locked with Val's. "Is that how you defend yourself? You lower the bar, so it's easier to step over?"

Now the Irishman sounded like an English snob. Val drained the whiskey and put his father's image out of his head. "We can both agree that I'm a cad. If I can find Rose someone who isn't like me, perhaps I'll have a slightly smaller stain on my soul."

O'Shea's eyes widened with an expression of sudden illumination. "Have you come here looking for a replacement?"

"I have," Val conceded.

The barkeeper's hands went up. Not in surrender. He had the look of someone who intended to stop a train with his bare hands. "Oh, no you don't. You aren't foisting an innocent lamb like Miss Muldoon off on the likes of me. I'm not interested in marriage. Take your business elsewhere."

Val breathed out a sigh. He couldn't work up disappointment. Just the opposite. But for Rose's sake, he had to try a little harder. Not only had O'Shea noticed her, he rightly viewed her as an innocent. The saloon owner had a good heart beneath that crusty surface. "But you could use the help, surely. You and Rose have much in common."

O'Shea gave a dry laugh. "And how would you know what we have in common? Other than an Irish heritage."

Again, he'd made a valid point. Val knew precious little about his wife's past. Most of what he'd come to believe had been based on assumptions. He knew even less about O'Shea's. Yet here he sat, playing matchmaker. For all he knew, Patrick O'Shea might be one of those who preferred his own kind. It didn't appear that way, but one couldn't always tell.

As for Rose, would she even want to live above a saloon?

"Top of the morning, Mr. O'Shea! And to you, Mr. Lord."

The greeting came from behind Val, a voice he recognized. He turned slightly to acknowledge the young man he'd encountered in the street the day before. If O'Shea could be considered muscular, this fellow resembled a pugilist. One with a barrel roughly the size of a small pig balanced on his shoulder.

"Mr. Childers, as I've explained, I am not a *lord*," Val said dryly.

"Well, that's good to know. You won't have to turn this into wine." Childers grinned at his joke and shifted his load onto the bar. *Fine Whiskey* had been imprinted on the side.

Val reserved the right to be suspicious of the claim. Most of the moonshine whiskey he'd tasted would be better applied as a tanning agent for leather. Taking into account the appearance of the distiller, it wasn't a stretch to assume this swill wouldn't be much better.

Mr. Childers hadn't donned the antiquated finery he'd worn yesterday, likely hoping to impress one of the women. Today, he'd taken only time enough to pull on a pair of patched bib dungarees and a yellowed shirt with the sleeves rolled back. His hair hung past his collar, a style that appeared to be less a decision and more the result of neglect.

Next to Childers, Rose looked like a lady of the manor.

The beefy young purveyor of moonshine held out his hand. "Congratulations for being the first man to get yourself one of them brides."

Val felt the press of hard callouses in the younger man's grip. Physical strength wasn't necessarily high on the list of traits, but a man who worked hard was better than a lazy one.

Childers patted the barrel. "This here is my best whiskey. Have Mr. O'Shea pour you a drink. It'll be on me."

The proprietor grumbled something unintelligible under his breath. He hauled the barrel behind the bar, as well as two other barrels Childers had brought in.

"Thank you, Mr. Childers," Val said.

"Call me Arch. Everybody does."

Generous. Friendly. Rose could do worse. As well, the young moonshiner looked closer to Rose's age. On the other hand, there was much to recommend maturity, thrift, and sobriety.

O'Shea placed Val's glass on the counter. Arch watched with a look of anticipation.

Val tasted the brew. "Very good." In fact, it was better than the expensive bottled whiskey he'd purchased earlier. He'd misjudged the man's abilities. What else might he have misjudged? "Do you plan to throw your name in the hat for a bride?"

O'Shea turned away, shaking his head and muttering.

"Haven't decided." Arch glanced toward the door. "I met your missus at the mercantile this morning. She rushed off to the land office before I got a chance to talk to her."

Val's protective instincts flared up. Why would a single young man initiate a conversation with a married woman? Unless he viewed boundaries like some horses viewed fences, to be leapt over. This would disqualify him immediately.

Something he said was equally bothersome. Why would Rose be rushing off to the land office? Unless Hardt had made advances already and had arranged a tryst.

Val issued a brusque thanks for the drink. "Good luck, Mr. Childers, if you decide to enter the bride lottery. And be advised, stay away from my wife."

⚘

Upon reaching the land office, Rose yanked open the door and lurched inside, breathing hard from having run the entire way.

Mr. Hardt, who'd been sitting behind his desk, jerked to his feet.

No one else was in the office.

"Mrs. Valentine, what's wrong?" He approached her, looking more concerned than angry.

"I..." She gasped for breath. Her heart hadn't stopped hammering. "It's sorry I am for bustin' in on you like this, but have you seen Val? I mean, Mr. Valentine?"

A dark look passed over Mr. Hardt's face but it was gone before she could decipher it. "He was here earlier. He left. Didn't say where he was going."

Her eyes stung. No, she couldn't go all weepy. She had to be strong and help her husband.

Rose swiped at her eyes. "At breakfast, Val said he was goin' out to take a look around his property. I have to find him. That man, can't recall his full name...Jarvis."

"Ned Jarvis?"

"That's him. He was in the store down the street, talking to another man—a young fellow—who he was trying to get to help him take revenge. When the bloke said no, he got mad and said he'd do it himself." Rose sucked in a breath and continued. "I don't know where he's gone. But I fear what he might do." She shivered and her chest tightened. "We got to find Val before that jack cove settles him."

Like the ruthless man who'd killed her father.

Mr. Hardt captured her hands and sandwiched them between his larger ones. "Calm down, Mrs. Valentine. Take deep breaths."

She sucked in air, following his firm directions. That did help clear her head.

"Now, tell me precisely what Mr. Jarvis said."

Rose started out speaking slower. "What he said was that Val stole his land and you helped him, and he wasn't letting either of you get away with it. He said he'd take care of it. And he was wearing a gun."

"Jarvis is a blowhard," Mr. Hardt said firmly. "But, just in case, I'll take his threat seriously. I'll speak to Lieutenant Goldman about the matter."

Coppers hadn't lifted a finger to help when her father had been knifed. Why would this army man be any different?

Rose shook her head. "What makes you think soldiers will do anything?"

"They're here to keep the peace. So far, the lieutenant has done a good job of it." Mr. Hardt patted the back of her hand. "Your safety is our utmost concern."

"It ain't me I'm worried about."

The door swung open. Her heart jumped into her throat as she swiveled her head, expecting to see an evil man with a gun. Instead, she met her husband's startled gaze.

Relief washed over her.

"Val!" She yanked her hand from Mr. Hardt's grip and ran to her husband, threw her arms around his neck, giddy with joy. "Saints be praised! Yer safe!"

He pulled her arms from around his neck. "Stay here," he ordered.

With explaining, he stalked over to where Mr. Hardt stood, hauled back his arm and punched the land agent in the face.

"No! Val! What are you doing?" Rose seized his arm before he could throw another punch.

Val couldn't shake off his wife to go after the rogue. Although he might not need to. The first punch had spun Hardt around and sent the bounder stumbling into his desk.

The land agent braced his weight on his arms A few drops of blood had spattered across a collection of papers strewn atop the desk.

Disorganized as well as being an adulterous bastard.

Rose clung to Val, babbling. Whatever she said couldn't penetrate the thick, hot cloud enveloping him. He'd heard men speak of a red haze or bloodlust, but he hadn't understood it until now. He wanted to tear Hardt apart with his bare hands.

Hardt straightened without a word. He braced his feet and clenched his hands, which he kept at his sides. For the moment. Blood oozed from one nostril. "What the devil is wrong with you?"

"Finding you holding hands with my *wife*. That's what's

wrong." Val tightened his fingers until his fists became mallets.

Rose stepped in front of him. "Val..." She cupped his face in her hands. Her smooth palms felt cool against his heated skin. "Look at me. Please. I was out of my mind with worry. Mr. Hardt was just tryin' to calm me down."

Val clenched his teeth. "Is that what you call it?"

"He was being kind," Rose insisted.

"I suppose you think the serpent was being kind to Eve, too." Val kept his gaze pinned to his opponent and wouldn't look Rose in the eye.

Reason told him this wasn't her fault. She was naïve and unsuspecting, besides being as transparent as glass. Like that sly snake in the garden, Hardt had noted her innocence and taken advantage of it.

Had Hardt thought he could get away with it because he assumed her temporary husband wasn't committed to protecting her? That misperception needed to be corrected. Immediately.

Val grasped his wife's hands and pulled them down, then he pushed her aside. "Go back to the hotel. We'll talk later." That was as much as he could manage without being harsh. He'd told her to stay put and she'd defied him.

She made a sound that might've been a sob, but when he looked, he saw no tears, only agony, twisting her features. "He didn't do anything wrong. Mr. Hardt was going to the lieutenant to get help—before you hit him. That man, Jarvis, I heard him make threats."

The name sent a cold chill down Val's spine. He grasped her arms. "When did you see Jarvis? Did he approach you?"

She shook her head. "I didn't even know it was Jarvis until I overheard him talking to some other man in the store. That's why I came to Mr. Hardt. I thought you might be out at your property, and I don't know where it is. I feared that horrid man would follow you and shoot you. I had to try to stop him."

Val's heart tripped. God forbid his wife would tangle with that miscreant. "Stop him? You stay away from him! Do you hear me?"

"Your husband is right. Stay away from Jarvis." Hardt's voice held that annoying authoritative tone, tinged with a hint of weariness. He'd retrieved a handkerchief and held it to his bleeding nose.

A twinge of guilt indicated to Val that his conscience had returned. He hadn't lost his temper like that since being taunted at school. In his rage, he'd dealt the bully a serious injury. After that, he'd avoided using his fists. But he hadn't thought twice before hammering Hardt's face. Fortunately, Hardt wasn't a small man or a weak one. Although his nose might've become weaker.

"Broken?" Val inquired.

"Not sure yet." Hardt's steady gaze didn't waver, but he leaned against the desk for support. Oddly enough, he hadn't fought back.

Val had expected the other man to start swinging and would've welcomed the battle. The surly agent didn't strike him as a coward. That meant Hardt had chosen not to retaliate, which could be a sign of guilt—or firm control over his emotions. The kind of control Val envied as much as he despised it. His father was like that. Cold. Hard. Immovable. However, his father hadn't gone after another man's wife, so far as Val knew.

He gripped Rose's hand. No matter what she said, he couldn't trust that Hardt's intentions were pure. The best thing would be to keep her as far away from the land agent as possible. Until he left. After that, he couldn't do a damn thing about it. Hardt could come after Rose, seduce her...

Anger worked its way up to Val's neck and into his jaw. He

clamped down on the urge to turn around and charge Hardt, drive him over the desk and force him to fight.

Rose stroked her hand down his arm, a light, gentle touch. That got his attention as nothing else could have. "We should leave together."

He nodded, not trusting himself to speak. She was right, of course. He couldn't send her home alone, knowing Jarvis lurked out there somewhere and might harm her to get at him. He circled a protective arm around her waist and led her outside.

Later, he would deal with Hardt. When he wasn't in the mood to kill him.

Val walked arm-in-arm with Rose in silence while keeping a sharp lookout. Until his enemy was dealt with, his wife wouldn't be safe going anywhere without him. "A man named Childers said he spoke to you at the mercantile."

"Oh, that's the name I couldn't recall. He was with Ned Jarvis."

If Childers had been on the list, he would be marked off. For all Val knew, the young moonshiner had come into the saloon to spy on him.

"What exactly did Mr. Childers say to you?"

"*Good morning*. I didn't give him a chance to say much more. I got the impression he was trying to keep Mr. Jarvis out of trouble."

"Nevertheless, you need to stay away from both men."

Rose kept her gaze trained straight ahead.

Possibly she interpreted his concern as suspicion and petty jealousy or she remained upset at his violent reaction. He would try a different approach and let her know he'd keep his word about taking care of her. In case she feared there might be some change of plan. The two of them were in this together, after all.

"I've procured a drill to use to locate the coal deposits. If

I find any, our land will be worth a great deal. We'll both be rich."

"If money is all you care about, why did you attack Mr. Hardt?"

She somehow posed the question without making it sound like an accusation.

Val couldn't come up with a good reason. Jealousy wasn't rational, given the fact he intended to end their marriage. Rage couldn't be explained away, although he could beg her pardon for his woeful lack of control. "Yes, of course, you're right. As a gentleman, I shouldn't have brawled in front of you. I hope you'll accept my apology."

Rose shot him an incredulous look. "You haven't answered my question."

"No. I haven't got an answer." Other than to say he'd gone mad when he'd seen Hardt touching her, and that much she knew. The very idea that he'd be able to select his replacement was ludicrous. She would have to find another husband on her own. After he was gone.

When they reached the hotel, he held her hand tucked over his arm until he'd opened the door for her. Inside, delicious smells filled the air. He latched onto something they could talk about other than his jealous rage. "Someone's baking."

"Aye, my stomach knows it." Rose smiled, which did something to his stomach that had nothing to do with hunger.

"Rose! You're back." Mrs. Braddock appeared from the parlor. She glanced at Val with a disapproving look he couldn't interpret. When he'd come across her in the store, she'd also looked at him that way. Excitement returned to her face as she retrieved Rose's arm and led her into the parlor. "Come in here and see what I found."

Val followed, curious as to what wonder awaited.

Two dresses—a light blue traveling suit and a warm brown day dress—were draped over the back of the sofa. Complementary fabric, cut in wide sections, had been pinned to the hems, extending the garments' length.

"You didn't return, so I had to guess the size, but we can measure it properly now that you're here." Mrs. Braddock drew out a length of lace from a wide spool. "I'll use a strip of lace to cover the seam at the bottom and no one will be the wiser."

His wife's eyes brimmed with tears.

Val's gaze traveled down her shabby dress to the oversized boots and back up to her hands, which clutched a threadbare shawl. Something hard and remorseless landed a blow just beneath his breastbone.

*Of course, you fool.* That's what they'd been doing at the store, picking out dresses for Rose. He'd berated her for leaving the hotel when he ought to have realized she needed to go shopping and purchase new clothes to replace her tattered wardrobe. He should've told her she could pick out whatever she wanted. No, he should've gone with her.

He needed to apologize for being such an ass. He'd repeatedly wounded her tender heart and his behavior had been inexcusable. Not only was he a poor provider, but he was also a terrible husband, even as a temporary one.

That would change. From this moment on, he would do everything in his power to make her life easier and better so that when he left, she would be happy and content. He wouldn't be happy or content, but he had no right to be. Never had this been more apparent than it was now.

AFTER THE NOON MEAL, VAL ESCORTED ROSE BACK INTO town. He'd promised her they would spend the afternoon together before he set out for the property. It was the least he could do, considering how shabbily he'd treated her.

As they walked, he kept an eye out for Jarvis. He anticipated the sore loser would at some point strike back. Given his nature, sniveling and cowardly, he wouldn't attack out in the open. He'd sneak up. Val didn't believe he'd need the gun he had in his pocket, but he was glad it was there, all the same.

They passed men on foot, men on horseback, and men driving carts and wagons. Every one of them eyed Rose as if she were something rare and wondrous. They tipped their hats and many offered greetings.

She wrapped her shawl closer in a gesture that indicated nervousness. "I'm getting itchy with all this attention."

"They're admiring you."

"There aren't no other women out here for them to ogle. They're staring at me like I belong in a circus."

Val put his hand over her fingers, curled tight in the crook of his arm. "If I ever meet the men responsible for making you believe that, I will gladly rearrange their faces."

She laughed softly. "Might take some time. There's quite a few of them."

However amusing she thought his remark, he didn't find her response funny. That was another thing he could leave her with, extra confidence in her unique loveliness. She couldn't doubt he found her attractive. Now he would convince her that any man who had a good pair of eyes would find her attractive too.

When he reached the cross street, he turned her to face him so she would see his sincerity. "Get used to men looking at you, Rose. You're a beautiful woman. Once you have pretty things to wear, you'll feel like a beautiful woman."

She searched his eyes. Still doubting. "Are you being glib now?"

He regarded her straight-faced. "Does it look to you like I'm being glib?"

"No, but..."

"I'll have to convince you." He turned her to face the street and a total of four clapboard buildings. "Where shall we start? Our choices are endless."

"Hmm." She curled her finger at her chin as if the matter required a great deal of thought. "I do like Mr. Appleton's General Store. He's a friendly bloke."

"You wouldn't want to make me jealous," Val murmured near her ear.

She shot him a worried look. "Oh, Mr. Appleton isn't interested in me. He's sweet on Susannah."

"I'd rather not take the chance."

"Oh, you." She smacked Val on the arm, chastising him for teasing her, but a faint blush on her cheeks encouraged him.

"Why don't we try Middaugh's Dry Goods and Clothing?" He led her across the street, which ended up being easier than he thought it would be. All traffic stopped.

"Hey, how'd you get that woman?" a man called out.

"I married her," Val replied. "You'll have to find one of your own."

He felt proud having Rose on his arm, despite her ugly dress. It was something he could fix easily enough. Then she wouldn't feel so self-conscious and have to wrap that worn shawl around her. He opened the door to the store and followed her inside.

She stopped and lifted her nose. "I love how it smells in here, like wool and linen. When I washed other folk's new clothes, the smell would come off them."

Rose had been a laundress. Something about her he hadn't known because he hadn't bothered to ask. He wanted to learn more while at the same time he didn't. The less he knew about her life, the easier it would be to let her go.

"Shall we see what they have?"

She looked at him askance. "I'll warn you. They won't have dresses long enough."

"Then we'll look at fabrics and have a dress made."

The proprietor behind the counter glanced over, saw Rose, and immediately left his customer and came their way. "Morning, folks. I'm Charlie Middaugh. May I help you, Mr...?"

"Valentine," Val supplied. "My wife needs some fabric. And we'd like to get the name of a seamstress."

Middaugh shook his head. "Know a tailor. We don't have any dressmakers in town. Not unless one of the women who arrived yesterday knows how to sew."

Rose looked at Val with a hopeful expression. "I can sew some. And Susannah says she's a good seamstress. She could help me."

"I'll pay Mrs. Braddock to make you a dress."

They followed Middaugh to the tables where rich wool, light cotton, and bright calico were wrapped on bolts. "Take your time," he said. "Let me know if you need anything."

Rose did take her time. She touched each fabric with reverence and appeared enraptured as she rubbed the cloth between her finger and thumb. Her utter bliss in choosing fabric, something the women he knew would take for granted, puzzled him.

"How long has it been since you've had new clothes?"

"My mother took in her dresses for me."

That explained why the garments were too short.

He felt a tug at his heart. Not pity—this was stronger, almost violent. "No one has ever purchased a dress just for you?"

Her expression turned oddly apologetic. "Are you angry we bought those readymade dresses on your credit?"

He stared at her, surprised. That's what she thought he meant? "No, I'm not angry with you. I'm angry with myself. I should've had the foresight to take you shopping."

Rose looked relieved. "That's all right. I didn't mind waiting."

In other words, she hadn't expected him to be thoughtful. Why should she? He'd told her he was leaving her, hadn't seen to her basic needs and he'd attacked a man she thought was helping her. He'd never felt more ashamed.

He spied a lady's straw hat on display nearby. Adorned with pink and white lace and silk red roses, it was pretty and feminine without being overly fussy—like Rose. Lifting it with care, he positioned it on his wife's head and tied the lace ribbon to one side of her chin. Then he took hold of an oval mirror on a stand and held it up.

He grinned at the awestruck joy that lit up her face. "You like it?"

"Oh, Val, it's...it's beautiful!"

"If you like it, it's yours."

Doubt flickered across her face. "Are you sure? We can afford it?"

"Of course we can." He'd put it on credit or sell his pocket watch if he had to, but he would not leave until he'd purchased Rose a proper wardrobe. "Every lady needs a hat."

Her delighted smile took his breath away.

"I've never had a pretty hat. Always wore scarves or my mum's bonnets. I can't thank you enough." She turned her head to look from other angles.

He moved the mirror obligingly. He'd bought hats for women before but never had he taken such pleasure in the gift or been so humbled by gratitude.

Rose took nothing for granted. He'd taken everything for granted—even her.

He set the mirror aside and gathered her hands. "I want you to have nice things."

The adoration she showered on him made his stomach clench. Thankfully, he would be gone before she discovered he wasn't God.

Her smile wavered. "I wish I could give you something."

"You have."

"What are you talking about? I haven't given you anything."

"For one, the pleasure of your company. Happiness at seeing your joy. Pride in showing off a beautiful wife. And a brand new perspective. Because of you, I'm learning to be grateful."

Her lips parted and her eyes widened in amazement.

"Those are the things you've given me just today."

She curled her fingers around his hands, a sweet trusting gesture. "If it's not too much, I'd like to ask for one more thing."

"I'll grant it. If it's in my power to do so."

Rose begged with her eyes. "Take me with you to look at the property."

The mere suggestion sent his pulse racing off at a gallop. Safety aside, he couldn't be alone with his wife for several days. Not even for a single night. He would ruin her, then he'd abandon her, and then he would have fallen lower than he had ever fallen in his miserable life. This was one request he couldn't grant even if it meant going back on his word.

"I'm sorry, I can't risk your safety. You must wait for me here, in town. With luck, I'll be gone less than a week." He squeezed her hands and placed an affectionate kiss on her forehead so she wouldn't think he didn't want to be with her.

He wanted that very much. Too much. "While I'm away, have Susannah make you a dress befitting a lady."

"Be-fitting a lady," Rose echoed. An unhappy look returned to her eyes. "Aye, that's what I'll do then, while you're gone. I'll work on being fitting."

"That's not—" He stopped before he embarrassed her for misunderstanding the meaning of his words. Her lack of education wasn't her fault. He suspected she'd be quick to learn. He longed for the opportunity to share the knowledge he'd gathered, formal and otherwise, but nothing he taught her could prepare her for the rejection she'd encounter if he took her home. "Sweet Rose, you don't have to work at fitting in. Just be yourself and you'll be fine. Everyone here loves you just the way you are."

Her expression turned reproachful. "Not everyone."

## ❧ 12 ❧

Over the next two days, Rose took the opportunity to improve herself.

Susannah escorted her into the dining room, explaining as they walked. "At a dinner party, the most distinguished gentleman—in this case, let's pretend it's your husband—will escort the lady of the house—that's you—to her seat."

"Here is where you will sit." Susannah stopped near the middle of the table. "Your husband will sit opposite. If there are no servants to serve food, he will serve the plates, there at his right, and you will preside over tea and sauces."

"Sauces..." Rose repeated. She searched the forest of tableware to locate what Susannah had called a sauceboat.

She would become a fitting lady if it killed her—and it just might.

Her head throbbed after being crammed full of etiquette and protocol. At least it kept her busy while Val was away, drilling in search of coal on his property. She was dead certain he had the easier job.

Charm, attended by Delilah, and Prudence with Danny

acting as her escort, took their seats around the table. Susannah had insisted on having her son present so he could learn proper manners. The three ladies had asked to join in on the lessons, which Rose was sure had more to do with being entertained than learning.

Everyone save her seemed to know the appropriate customs and manners. Things Rose hadn't been taught. Oh, her mother had insisted on good behavior, but this was different. Some rules attached to being a lady were ridiculous. Keeping one's bonnet on in the house when visiting, but not if staying the night. Using one hand to lift the side of her skirt slightly above the ankle when crossing a street. Keeping the hem of a perfectly good dress out of the mud using *both* hands was considered vulgar rather than practical.

Rose stared in dismay at all the glassware and utensils. "Why are there so many glasses and forks and spoons and such? What's the sense in putting everything you own out all at once? Just means more to clean."

"Rose, honey, *you* won't be cleaning them," Delilah drawled.

"Your husband will employ kitchen staff," Prudence added. "If he can't afford servants, he won't be able to buy you all this." She indicated the tableware with a sweeping motion of her hand. "So you won't have to clean it."

The Illinois farm girl had both knowledge and practicality. Rose admired both. She also envied Prudence's skills in the kitchen, which she'd demonstrated by helping Mrs. Fry with the refreshments for Rose's wedding as well as cooking most of the evening meals.

It seemed to Rose that the hotel owner might be taking advantage of Prudence's good nature, but when she'd mentioned it, Prudence had brushed off the concern and said she welcomed the opportunity to show off her skills. Being plain, she declared, wouldn't matter after the men tasted her cooking.

"Whether or not you have servants is beside the point," Susannah said. "Given Mr. Valentine's background and family, you'll be attending dinner functions and hosting them. You'll want to know proper etiquette to avoid embarrassment."

Susannah spent the next hour explaining which things were used for what. Proper table manners. The things you could talk about, like weather, and the things you shouldn't talk about, like politics.

"The discussion of emotional topics at dinnertime upsets digestion," she explained.

Rose scratched her head in confusion. "Da always had a good appetite when he got wound up over politics."

"Political intrigue does tend to get the stomach juices flowing," Charm acknowledged.

"It is also impolite to talk about bodily functions at the dinner table," Susannah added with a sharp look at the offender.

"And don't forget, avoid sneezing, coughing, and—" Charm scrunched her nose and waved her hand in front of it. "Expelling gas."

Danny went into a fit of laughter.

His mother pushed back her chair and stood. "Let's move on to other topics."

Rose restrained the urge to laugh along with Danny. It would ease some of her tension. She scooted her chair back. Upon Susannah's pointed look, she realized she should've waited for her *husband* to assist her. "How about something fun. Like dancing?"

They'd no sooner moved the furniture aside than someone knocked at the door. Mrs. Fry went to answer and returned with a soldier in tow.

"Ladies, this is Lieutenant Goldman."

Had Rose not clapped eyes on Val first, she would've said the sandy-haired officer was the most handsome man she'd seen since her arrival. He didn't exceed her in height, but he appeared taller because he stood so straight.

This must be the soldier Mr. Hardt had mentioned. The one who'd done a good job of keeping the peace. What had brought him here?

"Lieutenant, may I introduce Mrs. Valentine, Mrs. Braddock, Miss Walker, and..." Their hostess hesitated. "This is Miss Bodean."

Delilah murmured a greeting. She kept her head down with her scarred cheek turned to the wall. The officer's gaze lingered, becoming speculative.

He'd noticed Delilah's beauty. Only a blind man wouldn't. How would he react if he saw the ravaged side of her face? Even if he wasn't unkind, she still wouldn't want him gawking at her.

Rose broke the awkward silence. "How can we help you, Lieutenant?"

The officer removed his hat. "You are Mrs. Valentine? Could you tell me where I might find your husband?"

Rose hesitated. Asking what business the officer had with her husband would be considered impolite, but making sure he wasn't in trouble was more important than being polite. "He's out at his claim. Is there something I should tell him?"

"We've detained a man who threatened to kill him and Mr. Hardt.

The blood left Rose's face. "Ned Jarvis?"

Susannah put her arm around her son's shoulders, drawing him closer. Concern was reflected on every face in the room.

"I didn't tell you this to worry you," Lieutenant Goldman continued. "We've got Mr. Jarvis locked up. I wanted to speak to your husband to obtain his statement."

What good would that do if Jarvis sent one of his friends after Val?

"Could you assign soldiers to protect Mr. Valentine?"

"I'm sorry, ma'am. My men are spread too thin to provide personal protection to individuals."

Rose bit her lower lip. She hated the thought of Val being out there alone.

The officer's stern countenance softened. "If it will put your mind at ease, I'll stop by and check on him."

"It would ease my mind, thank you."

Lieutenant Goldman gave a slight nod. "Pleased to be of service."

"Yes, that is very thoughtful of you, Lieutenant." Susannah let go of Danny and stood. "Would you happen to know the quadrille?"

The officer eyed her quizzically. "Yes, ma'am. I'm familiar with the quadrille."

"And the waltz?"

"That too."

"What about the polka, the gallop?"

Rose smiled broadly after recovering from her surprise. *Finally*. A man Susannah found interesting. And good for her, she wasn't letting proper manners stand in way of getting to know him.

The lieutenant appeared to catch on at the same moment. He fiddled with the corded hatband and seemed a bit nervous or maybe he was shy. At least he didn't turn and run. "Yes, Mrs. Braddock, I know how to dance."

"Excellent. Could you spare a few minutes to partner with Mrs. Valentine and help us teach her some of the steps? She's eager to learn, but I'm a poor substitute for her husband."

*That's* why Susannah wanted him to stay?

The lieutenant's sandy eyebrows arched. He'd been equally surprised. But he stopped toying with his hat and his tense posture relaxed. Every sign pointed to relief. "It would be my pleasure."

Rose heaved a disappointed sigh. Those two would've made pretty children.

She went along with her friend's suggestion, not because she was interested in dancing with the lieutenant. She'd rather dance with her husband. First, she had to learn the steps along with all the table rules so she could behave fitting a lady and convince him to keep her.

Come to think of it, if she learned quick enough she could go out to find him and demonstrate her newfound skills and make sure he was safe at the same time.

## 13

"Thank you ever so much for the ride!" Rose waved to the farmer as he turned the mule team around and drove them up the narrow, rutted road they'd just come down.

Lord, she was glad to be out of that wagon. Her insides felt rearranged by the constant jolting. With a deep breath, she gathered her courage, hefted her new satchel, and set off down a footpath carved through the waist-high prairie grass. According to the farmer, the stalks would grow to her shoulders before summer ended. She'd never seen grass so tall.

This path led to the house Val had been living in for more than a week. He'd told her he would be drilling to collect samples, looking for coal—his black gold. He could've taken a day to come see her, but he hadn't. He was avoiding her.

She had done as he'd asked and waited although each day dragged into the next, made all the worse by her longing for him. Did he long for her? Had she invaded his thoughts a thousand times a day as he had hers? Regardless, she refused to be ignored any longer. She wouldn't convince him to take her home with him if they were never together. With Ned

Jarvis locked up, things had calmed considerably. Surely he wouldn't begrudge her a wee visit.

Rose breathed in the rich, earthy fragrance. She ran a gloved hand over the tops of the slender, swaying stalks, which later in the summer would bloom purplish-blue. *Turkey Foot*, the farmer had called it, aptly named for the grass's three-pronged tops. Prairie chickens and songbirds loved the seeds. Overhead, a red-tailed hawk circled perhaps to see whether the intruder might be something tasty, then flew off in search of smaller prey.

One could understand why the posters called this land Paradise. It looked untouched since the dawn of creation.

The path took a turn and the leafy tops of trees became visible over the grass. Mr. Sprouse had told her the homestead was built near a creek, and she'd know she was getting close when she saw the post oaks.

Her heart beat faster. She picked up her pace, having no problem walking in the new shoes she'd obtained, thanks to the kind shopkeeper.

She couldn't wait to show off what she'd learned. More than that, she wanted to show Val how much she missed him and turn this pretend marriage into a real one. Now that she'd become a lady, he would have no reason to leave her behind.

The grass ended at a clearing.

Rose frowned at the sight greeting her. That wasn't a house. It was a tarpaper box with a slanted roof covered with more tarpaper. Nothing grew in the bare dirt around the shanty, although it appeared someone had started a garden of rubbish. It wasn't as bad as the garbage overflowing the alley behind the apartment building in Five Points, but the refuse looked obscene out here in this pristine wilderness.

Walking past the trash, she looked askance at a pile of cans that, according to the labels, had contained beans. Was that all her husband had been eating? She'd been feasting like royalty in comparison.

"Val?" she called out. Her voice bounced back from a nearby line of trees where he'd parked a wagon that held what looked like a load of rocks and dirt.

As she got closer, she could see beneath the seat his drills and shovels and what looked like a large blade that might fit a plow. The horse stood off in a field of shorter grass, grazing contentedly.

Her husband had to be around here somewhere.

"Hello? Val?" Rose approached the door, little more than a wooden frame with more tarpaper held up by leather hinges. Her hand trembled as she reached for a piece of rope hanging from a small hole. She assumed it was attached to a latch inside.

There were other dangers besides Mr. Jarvis. Thieves. Wild animals. Or Val might've come down ill.

A flock of birds burst from the trees, twittering. Fear gripped her heart when she saw something move within the grove. A shadow appeared before the dark form became a man.

She caught a sharp breath as Val emerged from the trees.

He didn't see her because he was looking down at the ground, lost in thought. His trousers hung low on his hips, suspenders dangling, and he carried his shirt slung over his shoulder. His jet black hair dripped water on his bare shoulders.

What a sight to behold!

She curled her fingers, eager to explore the sprinkling of dark hair across his chest, follow the line that arrowed down his abdomen, and discover the secrets he'd hidden from her. "Val?" Her voice came out rough with yearning.

He looked up and halted, staring at her like she was a

ghost. Dark bristles covered the lower half of his face. The half-grown beard gave him a rakish handsomeness.

"Rose?" His voice quavered, and an answering shiver ran through her.

She dropped her satchel and raced to meet him. He met her halfway. As she threw her arms around his neck, he lifted her by the waist. Their mouths collided.

He kissed her with the frantic desperation of a man who'd been deprived of the essentials in life, like food and water, holding her so close not even a blade of grass could fit between them.

The kiss went from awkward to searching to deeply satisfying. She had hoped he'd be pleased to see her, but his reaction exceeded her dreams. He couldn't kiss her like this and still want to let her go. Her heart soared as high as those birds winging into the sky.

What brought her back to earth were the rough bristles on his face burning her skin. She drew away and reached up to his jaw, running her fingers over the stiff, half-grown beard. "I like the way it looks more than the way it feels."

He blinked like she'd cracked him on the head. His dark brows gathered in a frown before he grasped her arms and moved her away. "What are you doing out here?"

"Coming to see you." She wound her arms around his neck.

He removed her hold on him with a flicker of regret in his eyes. "It's not safe for you to be here. Go home."

Oh no, she'd not let him push her away, not after that kiss.

Rose placed her hands on his chest, an alluring contrast of soft hair and hard muscles that quivered at her touch. "You needn't worry about Mr. Jarvis anymore. He got put in jail after he bragged to half the town that he was going to kill you and Mr. Hardt. Didn't Lieutenant Goldman come by? He said he'd tell you."

Val backed up a step, drew on his shirt, and, sadly, buttoned it. "He did tell me and said you'd asked him to stop by. I told him to tell you I was fine and not to worry."

"That he did, but it's not worry that brought me out here."

Val's gaze shifted over her shoulder in the direction of the shanty, and weary disappointment pulled at his features. "Even so, this place isn't suitable."

He'd started backing away, making excuses again. She hadn't even gotten the chance to demonstrate all she'd learned.

"Look, I have something to show you. Remember this fabric you picked out?" She lifted one side of the calico skirt and made a twirl, slow enough to show off the bustle in the back.

The pretty pattern, creamy daisies in between bands of green and brown, complimented her coloring. Especially her hair, or so said her friends.

"So? What do you think? Susannah helped me make it, and I've got a proper..." She searched for a polite word for the horsehair contraption strapped to her backside. "Unmentionable."

She wiggled her hips to make the point.

To her relief, that brought on a smile. "You certainly did."

He took her gloved hand and rubbed his thumb over the soft cotton, then lifted her arm for another pirouette. When she came back around, his eyes glowed with a look that said he was well pleased. "The dress is made more lovely by the wearer."

Her heart did a happy dance.

"Thank you, sir." She executed a curtsy. "As you can see, I've been learning."

"Learning?" He arched an eyebrow. "What have you been learning?"

"Oh, loads. Look." She turned and glided toward the shack, keeping her shoulders straight while swinging her hips slightly. "And I've taken to wearing gloves everywhere. They get dirty so I have to wash them at night."

She halted at the edge of a fire pit. The gray ashes had been cold for some time. An industrious spider had woven a web across the opening of a pot filled with leaves.

Regret squeezed her chest. She'd been well fed and comfortable while he'd been out here living in a tarpaper shanty with no one to see to it that he had healthy meals or clean clothes. What good did it do her to learn to be a proper lady when she wasn't even given the chance to be a proper wife?

Rose executed another turn and nearly ran into him, not realizing he'd followed.

A crease marred his brow. "You look very pretty, but you shouldn't be here, Rose. I expressly told you to wait for me—"

"You haven't shown me around yet." Rose darted past him and set off for the shack. Her stomach tightened with nervousness. He'd already told her he was leaving as soon as he sold his land. If she couldn't stay here to convince him she'd become a lady, she'd lose her chance to change his mind.

She flung open the door to the shanty and walked in. A musty smell struck her at the same time as the heat. The sun shining on that black tarpaper would turn this shack into an oven by the time late summer rolled around. Surely Val would be long gone by then, and she intended to go with him so they wouldn't be suffering for long.

The walls were lath and partially covered with newspaper, mostly in spots where the wind had torn away strips of tarpaper on the outside. Light shone through the boards in several places illuminating a bare dirt floor and meager furnishings, including a cot that was little more than branches nailed together with a thin mattress thrown on top. The blanket, at least, looked clean. Crates served as shelves on which were stacked various containers and cans. Window openings had oilcloth nailed over them.

This place needed airing out and cleaning.

Rose smoothed her hands over her brand new dress. Not at all the right clothing for out here. She would've brought her old work dress if Susannah hadn't taken it away and hidden it somewhere—or maybe she'd burned it.

Val pushed the door wide and propped it open with a large rock, letting in light and a blessed breeze. He crossed the room, ducking beneath a crossbeam—if he stood up straight, his head would bump the ceiling. "You came out here to show me your dress?"

No, she came out here to save her marriage.

"You think I'm silly?"

"I don't think you're silly. But I'll think you're mad if you still want to stay now that you've seen this place."

Rose refused to be drawn into an argument. She was staying, and that was that. Venturing closer, she reached up and combed her fingers through his damp hair, tucking the lengthening strands over his ear and letting him know with a look how much she sympathized. "I'll be here to help ye, Val, so it'll go easier."

His fingers locked around her wrist and he drew her hand down. It hurt that he kept pushing her away even though he needed her. "You cannot stay out here, Rose. This shack isn't fit for hogs."

Rose released an irritated breath and drew off her gloves. Impressing on him that she was now a lady had put her at a surprising disadvantage when it came to being a helpmate. If she opened his eyes to her past, it wouldn't impress the aristocrat, but it would ease the conscience of the struggling landowner. "You remember I promised for better or worse? Well, I've lived with worse than this."

His mouth tipped up in that stomach-tickling half-smile. "Worse than dirt?"

"Some filth is worse than dirt." She struggled for a way to describe the squalor without painting a picture that would disgust him. "I grew up in a poor neighborhood. You'd call it a slum. Five Points. I imagine that wouldn't mean anything to you."

The horrified look on his face told her differently. "If you mean Five Points in New York City, then, yes, I'm familiar with it. I spent some time in New York before I headed out west. I can't believe you lived in that place. It's worse than Devil's Acre in London."

Rose knew nothing about the Devil's Acre, but the name was enough to make plain it was a bad place. Well, then. He ought to realize she could deal with dirt. She didn't want to dwell on her poverty any longer than necessary—it only made the differences between them more glaring. At the same time, she was grateful to him for lifting her out of it.

She rubbed her thumb over the soft cotton gloves in her hand. "I never had nice things like these gloves or this dress. I can't thank you enough for them."

"You don't owe me thanks." His voice dropped to a low register the way it did when he grappled with strong emotions. "A husband provides for his wife."

"My da worked whatever jobs he could get to provide for us. He didn't make much, though, and we had a big family." Grief thickened in her throat. "For a while, we had a big family."

Val stepped closer. She hoped he might put his arms around her, but then he reached up and cupped his hand on a beam. The shanty, poor as it was, didn't need his help to remain upright, so he must've grabbed something to keep from touching her. That's what his eyes were saying, anyway. "Tell me about them."

"My family?" She took a breath. Her story might be more than he wanted to hear, but she was glad he seemed interested. He'd asked so few questions about her past. "We immigrated from Ireland during the potato famine. I was a wee sprout, so I don't remember the auld country. My older brother did. Da never got over missing it. He was a farmer there. Over here, he built roads. Mam took in laundry and mending. Being the eldest girl, I helped her and watched the little ones. That's why I never finished school."

"What happened to them?"

Rose hesitated. She didn't like talking about that part because it brought back the aching loss. "You got enough to worry about. You don't need to hear my tale of woe."

"Maybe not, but I think you need to tell it." His gaze grew intimate, caring, urging her to trust him. Could be he was right and it might hurt less if she shared it. With him being her husband, these were things he should know.

"Da was murdered...over two dollars." Her stomach knotted as it always did whenever she thought about her father's senseless death. "He was so stubborn. He wouldn't give it up. They stabbed him."

"That's why you were so afraid for me," Val mused. "You thought Jarvis would kill me if I didn't give him his deed."

She gave a slow nod.

"We'll come back to that. Go on."

"Tom, my older brother, died in the war." She lifted her chin. "We were all so proud of him. He served with the Irish Brigade. Fell at Gettysburg."

"I heard about their bravery." Val's respectful tone encouraged her to go on.

"Oh, aye. We sang songs about it. I could sing one to you later. 'Tis a bonny tune." She tried to put on a brave face.

"You had younger siblings?"

"Four." Her voice wavered. "This is hard to talk about."

"Take your time."

Rose closed her eyes and had to swallow her tears before she could speak. "Cholera broke out in sixty-six. Michael, Kathleen, and Bridget got sick. Mam tried everything. Dosed them with healing teas, bathed them, prayed the rosary over them. We couldn't afford medicine, and the doctors wouldn't come into the neighborhood."

She took a sharp breath. Had to finish before she broke down. "This past March, Mam and my youngest brother, Willy, died in a fire. It happened early in the morning while I was out collecting laundry. When I came back, the place was all in flames. The coppers pushed us back and wouldn't let us through. I had to stand on the corner and watch the building burn, and I couldn't do a thing. Not a single, bloomin' thing."

He dragged her up against him, holding her tight. "Sweet Rose, go ahead and cry. Let it out. You've been carrying too heavy a load. That kind of grief will drown you."

Yes, she had been drowning, and he had plucked her out of the cold water.

Rose buried her face in his shoulder, grabbed the back of his shirt, and hung on for dear life. She wept tears of grief for her family and tears of gratitude for a kind and caring husband she didn't deserve. When she drew back, her face wet, he lifted the tail of his shirt and dried her tears.

"I'm sorry," she whispered. "For getting your shirt wet."

"It needed a good washing."

With a choked laugh, she went back into his arms. He stroked her back in comforting circles and toyed with the loose tendrils at her neckline. His gentle touch, his kindness, and understanding, his solid presence, and even his clean, masculine scent brought her comfort. When she was with him, she felt whole and at peace.

She pulled back with a relieved smile, sensing they'd turned a corner. "You're right. I did need to tell it, and I needed a good cry. I'm better. Now, let me look around for something I can put together for your dinner...besides beans."

The wry smile fell away. "You aren't staying."

Rose frowned at his stubborn insistence, confused and hurt by the conflicting messages he sent through his actions. "Why do you pull me close and then push me away?

A stricken look passed across his face. He took an abrupt step back, and his head struck the beam with a thump. "Ow," he muttered under his breath. Remaining hunched over, he cupped his hand to the hurt. She would've rubbed it, but he didn't let her get close enough.

"You haven't forgotten that I'm leaving?"

That old tune again?

"No, my memory is fine. I know you want to leave. But I thought you'd take me with you now that I've learned enough."

"Learned enough? For what?"

She shook her head, surprised and a little sad that he hadn't figured it out yet. "For *you*. I know you need a lady wife, so that's what I learned to be. Your lady wife."

He stared down at her, but his expression didn't reflect the pleasure or even the tenderness she'd seen before. He looked distressed. Maybe even a little horrified.

"It's all right. I know I'm not a real lady yet. I'll get better at it."

The emotions that flickered across his face were hard to decipher, and then they were gone, shuttered behind a mask. "You don't have to learn anything, not for me. Believe me the effort isn't worth it."

If he'd thrust a knife through her chest, it couldn't hurt worse. What was he saying? That no matter how hard she tried, she could never learn enough? Never be good enough for him? The truth crushed her hope.

Oh, he might be attracted to her, even feel sorry for her, seeing her desperation, but she'd been fooling herself into thinking she could mold herself into the kind of woman he wanted.

Unable to face him without dissolving into another embarrassing bout of tears, she dodged past him and fled out the door.

## 14

He deserved to be horsewhipped. How many times would he hurt Rose before he learned not to put his hands or his lips anywhere on her person?

Val scrubbed his fingers through his hair, wincing when he encountered the egg he'd grown after backing into a cross-beam. That was the first time he'd whacked his head on the crossbeams, all because he'd been stupid enough to take Rose into his arms. Something he'd dreamed of doing last night and the night before and the night before that.

When he'd first seen her standing next to that dilapidated shack, looking so fresh and lovely, he'd thought she was an illusion. His brain hadn't started working again until well after they'd commenced kissing. If she hadn't pulled back to remark on his unshaven face, he might've swept her up and carried her into the woods and...

He swore under his breath. Letting his thoughts wander off in that direction wouldn't do either of them any good. Right now, he needed to do what he should've done in the first place. Take her back to town.

Turning, he collided with the crates he'd used as shelves.

Cans fell to the floor. Two rolled under the bed he'd pulled into the middle of the room to avoid the bugs that came out of the walls, especially at night. His skin prickled at the memory of waking up with something crawling up his arm. He wouldn't subject his wife to that or to an owl swooping down on her while she took care of her personal needs in the woods or to the countless other things he'd encountered out here. Including Indians. They'd been less frightening than the bugs.

Picking up the cans he could see, he slammed them on top of the crate and strode outside.

Rose stood over by the wagon. She couldn't make it clearer that she was ready to leave. What did he expect after he had abused her tender heart by saying her efforts to impress him weren't worth it? He'd meant to say *he* wasn't worth her efforts.

The admiration in her eyes when she'd looked at him had soothed his pride and filled his heart to bursting, but his conscience wouldn't let him accept it.

Her heartbreaking story, of how much she loved and missed her family, had stirred something deep inside. He longed to offer her more than a shirt she could soak. Except, he'd never experienced the kind of familial love she'd described, and he didn't know how to give. He knew only how to take. If she learned half the things he'd done, the selfishness that encrusted his heart, she wouldn't waste her time on him.

That's what he had to do. Abandoning her at the hotel would only make her believe he was rejecting her again. But if he told her about his sordid past, about why he had to leave and what drove him to return, she wouldn't want to remain with him. She'd be able to shed her infatuation and open her heart to someone more deserving.

His stomach twisted at the thought.

"Let me get the horse. I'll take you back." He would talk to her on the way to town. At least then he wouldn't have to look her in the eye while he confessed his sins.

"No, I don't think so."

Her rebellious remark arrested his retreat.

She turned around, holding one of the large drill bits. As she picked away pieces of grass stuck to the blades, her brow pinched in a thoughtful frown. "Before, you said we're in this together, so I'll be staying here to help you. Don't worry about me begging you to take me along. I won't ask again. But I'll not be shirking my duties in the meantime."

He started in her direction. "You are not shirking your duties because you don't owe me anything."

She dropped the bit back into the wagon and then crossed her arms over her chest in a gesture that bespoke defiance. "I made my vows. Even if they mean nothing to you, they mean something to me."

Her remark had the effect of a slap. She couldn't have insulted him more if she'd tried.

"This has nothing to do with our vows, which, by the way, I take very seriously. There's nowhere out here for you to stay. Only one bed. I'd give it to you, but you wouldn't want to sleep in it. The place is infested with bugs."

She marched over to the shack and picked up the satchel she'd left beside the door. "I've lived with bugs before. So big they could pick up a baby and carry it off. Bugs don't scare me. But if they scare you then you can sleep outside."

"Scare me? I'm not scared of..." He clamped his jaw shut before he told a lie. She'd change her tune after she met that insect with a million legs. Maybe it would do her good to sleep one night in the shanty. She'd be more than ready to leave in the morning. He could put a blanket under the wagon. There were probably fewer bugs under there than in the house.

"Suit yourself."

"Thank ye, I will." She opened the door and vanished inside.

He walked to the door and was met with a titillating view of her backside as she crouched down on all fours and peered under his bed. "What are you doing?"

"Just seeing how big the bugs be."

"They don't come out until dark. Usually."

She retrieved the missing can. "Do you have anything other than beans?"

He offered her a hand and helped her stand. "There's jerky, canned milk, canned peaches."

"Flour? Lard?"

What did she think she would find in here, a fully stocked kitchen?

"I don't cook."

"No, I don't suppose you do."

"Should I?"

Her shoulder lifted in a slight shrug. "You were born with a silver spoon in your mouth. So why would you know how to do such things as cooking." She took a meaningful look around the room. "Or cleaning."

Val straightened as much as the low ceiling would allow. "In case you hadn't noticed, the floor is dirt. You can't *clean* dirt."

She'd already turned away from him and went poking around behind crates.

"What are you looking for?"

"A broom." She found what she sought in a corner. "In case you hadn't noticed, you can sweep a hard-packed floor. That'll get some of the bugs out."

He stood aside as she whisked the small room, using the tip of the broom to get into the corners. She dislodged a few dead bugs. Small ones. Or did they just look smaller in the daylight? She swept them outside with a flourish. When she'd finished making her point, he took the broom. Bugs were the least of their problems.

"Walk with me down to the creek. We'll need fresh water, and you might enjoy the view." He would certainly prefer more pleasant surroundings when he confessed things that weren't so pleasant.

Val leaned the broom against an outside wall and then picked up a bucket he had forgotten to take when he went down earlier to wash off the dirt and sweat. He'd spent all day digging and drilling, but coming up with nothing. His impatience added to his frustration. Two hallmarks of his life that remained constant, even now.

Rose walked alongside him into the trees. Above their heads in the leafy canopy, birds sang. Two squirrels chattered and chased one another, leaping from branch to branch. Around their feet, wild violets bloomed in surprising profusion.

Val heard the creek gurgling before it came into view. The peaceful surroundings eased some of the tension in his chest and shoulders. Her arm brushed his and the tension returned, only this time centered in the nether regions.

"I saw rocks and dirt in the wagon. Have you found coal yet?" she asked.

"No. But I still have another section to sample." He tried not to sound discouraged. Based on the sympathetic look she gave him, he failed.

"You're worried you won't find any."

"For your sake, I hope that's not the case."

"Why do you say, for my sake?"

"Because I want to leave you wealthy enough to live in comfort."

Her expression turned reproachful. "I don't need much to be comfortable. Being wealthy isn't important to me."

Given the grinding poverty in her past, it should be.

"It's important to me that you have the resources to live without worry."

She stood a few feet back while he squatted by a spot where the water flowed clear. "I'm not the worried one. And as much as I appreciate you wanting to take care of my material needs, I don't think this is about me."

Rose already saw through him to a degree so he might as well conquer his cowardice and expose his true nature.

"You're right. I am worried. I'm concerned I won't make enough to take care of you and to replace what I've wasted."

She remained quiet for a moment and then spoke. "You spent all your money?"

"And a fair amount of my father's money. Gambling, betting on horses, drinking like a fish, entertainment, women... At one point, I convinced my younger brother to join me in my excesses and managed to ruin him as well."

Val kept his attention focused on the task of filling the bucket because he didn't want to see the expression on Rose's face. Her father had been murdered for two dollars. She'd be repulsed by his careless, wasteful life.

"Why would you do that?"

Leave it to Rose to boil it down to one simple question. One he didn't want to answer.

"Because it was fun?" Val set the bucket aside, fighting to overcome his fear and self-loathing. He owed her more than a flippant reply. "I'm impetuous, selfish and destructive. At least, that's what I've been told for as long as I can remember. As it turns out, it appears they were right."

"They?"

He stood but still couldn't force himself to face her directly. "My parents, my governesses. I went through an astonishing number before I was sent off to school. The teachers tried their best to beat the devil out of me, but they had no luck. Neither did my older brother nor my former betrothed, although she employed kinder methods."

"Sounds to me like you wanted to prove them right."

"In part. But you see, that only confirms their perceptions. Otherwise, I wouldn't have done it. My misspent youth is the reason I'm here in America. The Baron purchased a one-way ticket and told me not to come back. But I've never minded him. Not once."

Rose drew closer. He couldn't see her standing behind him, but he knew she was there. Her nearness set off thrumming energy that charged his nerves and heightened his senses. It didn't feel the same as the forceful agitation that had caused him to break things and hurt people when he was younger. This powerful surge tugged at his very soul. He longed to embrace the source, though he was terrified of what might happen if he did.

Her fingers curled around his arm. She held onto him with both hands. Was she worried she might lose her way? If so, he was the very last person she should hold onto.

"Tell me why you must go back."

Another question he'd been waiting for, and dreading.

"To salvage my wretched pride." He knew now that wasn't possible. Ironically, Rose had taught him that. Going home rich wouldn't prove anything, and he would feel no better about himself.

Everything he'd done since he'd arrived in America, including marrying Rose, only confirmed he was still impetuous and selfish, and he had destroyed too many lives. He'd nearly ruined hers, but she had such amazing resilience that would bounce back.

One day, after she found a good husband and had a house full of children to look after and love, he would be nothing more than a bad memory.

## 15

Rose stayed the night, as she'd vowed to do. She wouldn't try to make herself into something she wasn't just to please him, she wouldn't walk away either. In the end, he might still leave, but retreating now would gain her nothing.

Val slept outside and gave her his bed, for all the good it did her. She didn't sleep a wink, which had nothing to do with the spiders and centipedes—a minor annoyance. However, she tucked away the fact that her husband feared them, even if he wouldn't admit it.

He hated showing weakness. He'd been mortified to have to make his confession to her and explain his penance.

*Impetuous. Selfish. Destructive.*

He didn't see those were just words—words used against him. She'd heard the same words to describe her youngest brother, Willy. Her parents hadn't called him those things, but just about everybody else did, and they said he ought to be punished. Instead of beating or berating him, her mother had done her best to keep Willy's energy focused, so he wouldn't get into trouble. Val's parents hadn't understood their son, even with all their learning. If they'd loved him, they hadn't shown it. He believed—and became—the terrible person he'd been told he was, and now he punished himself for it. He didn't need more punishment. He needed love, yet he wouldn't accept it. The knotty problem had kept her up all night.

In the morning after Val left, Rose cleaned up and aired out the shanty. She unearthed a surprise behind the dwelling, the remains of a garden with carrots and potatoes. Using some canned milk, she made up a nice soup. As evening approached, she heated their meal.

Drawing her skirt away from the edge of the fire pit, she leaned over to add salt to the pot and stir the soup. The fragrant smell wafted upward and she smiled with satisfaction. Her mother always said men were much easier to get along with when they were well fed.

"Rose!" The excitement in Val's tone was evident even over the distance. The tall grass shook and parted as he drove the horse through it. No sooner had the wagon rolled to a stop than he jumped out and ran in her direction. His broad smile told her something good had happened while he'd been out drilling. Something wonderful.

Before she could form the question, he seized her by the waist and twirled her around twice before setting her on her feet and bending down for a kiss.

She returned the unexpected gift in full measure, giving as well as she got, pouring everything in her heart into the kiss.

Her pulse sped up when he drew her closer, deepening the intimacy. His lips explored hers, his tongue doing things that made her tremble and his touch igniting the sweetest ache. When he ended the kiss, she gasped.

She'd forgotten to breathe.

He stared at her as if he'd never seen her before. Or

maybe he'd been as affected by that kiss as her. Her head still spun, and she couldn't put two words together.

Abruptly, he crushed her against him. "Rose," he whispered in her ear. "I've found it... Coal."

She regarded him with loving amusement. "Such sweet words, dear husband. You know how to flatter a girl."

One corner of his mouth curled upward and she felt the pull on her heartstrings. "Oh, I'm not done yet. Let me show you."

He took her by the hand and led her over to the wagon. More dirt and rocks, but these rocks were black. Reaching into the bed, he withdrew one and offered it to her as a gentleman might offer flowers.

She turned the black, pitted gift over in her hands. "Looks like a black rock."

Val bent over, his forehead nearly touching hers. "Oh, no, not just a rock do I offer you. That is steam coal, my lady."

He cupped her face in his palms and tipped her chin, dropping a kiss on her nose before he brushed her lips with a feather-light touch. Before she could respond, he drew back, his mouth and eyes conveying reluctant resignation. "Coal is a much better gift."

"I'll be the judge of that." She reached up and threaded her fingers through his hair, over his ear. "Did you lose your hat?" Her hand moved down his neck to his shoulders, where black suspenders hugged a sweat-dampened shirt. "Befuddled man," she murmured. "You left your coat somewhere as well. Your vest is safe, though. It's clean and folded up."

Her heart ached for him to accept her, to let her show him how loveable he was, even when he forgot things or got distracted or impatient. He also put boots on a poor girl's feet like they were fine slippers and made her believe she could be beautiful and desirable. He fought for her and protected her and put his arms around her when she needed comfort. Was it any wonder she'd fallen head over heels in no time at all?

She fingered a loose button on his shirt. "Ah, Val, who'll look out for you, if not me?"

He fondled loose strands of her hair. Then he dropped his hand. "I wouldn't volunteer for the job if I were you."

His teasing tone couldn't hide his pain. He couldn't shield it from her, not anymore. Yet he refused to let her in so she could help heal what was hurt inside him. He'd keep pushing her away until he pushed her out of his life.

Desperate, she leaned closer and ran her finger along his smooth jaw. The muscles tightened at her touch. Encouraged by his response, she kissed his chin. "Did you shave this morning so your beard wouldn't scratch me?"

He went still. His crystal-light eyes glittered with agonized desire. "Don't tempt me, Rose. Let me leave with at least that much of my honor intact."

The hope she'd nurtured withered further. Soon, it would die. Even so, she couldn't keep it alive by manipulating him. She took a step back and smoothed her skirts with a steadying breath. "Aye, you're right. I want to be with you, Val, but I want it to be what you want as well. It's sorry, I am, for tempting you."

"Rose, I do want..." He stepped closer but stopped short of touching her. "I want you more than I've ever wanted any woman. The reasons I can't be with you are due to my sins, not yours."

"Love covers a multitude of sins." The phrase she'd heard her mother recite popped into her head and out of her mouth. She hadn't understood it—until now. "I know sins can't be ignored, Val, but they can be set aside. Covered up. You don't have to go back to them or let them get in the way of living. You just have to be willing to let love do its work."

He blinked down at her, seeming startled by what she'd said, but then he turned away and began to unhitch the mule.

If he'd stop hating himself for just a minute, he might see that he didn't have to keep piling on the punishment.

She curled her hands into fists, tempted to pound on him, or as her Da would say, knock some sense into him. "Did you hear me? *I love you*, Val. I don't care what you've done. If you haven't asked for forgiveness, go to confession. Say you're sorry. That's all you have to do. It's all you *can* do. Going back and trying to make up for the past won't change anything."

He turned, his face stripped of defenses—his pain, his agony, his shame, all there for her to see. "Don't love me, Rose. Don't make that mistake. I'm not the kind of man you can depend on. Even if I don't fail you now, at some point I will. It's what I do. I disappoint people and let them down. I hurt them. *That's* why I have to leave."

VAL TOOK THE QUICKEST ESCAPE ROUTE, A TRIP TO THE creek under the pretense of washing up. He had to get away to regain his composure before he gave in to this desperate need to hold Rose...and keep holding her.

He dropped to his knees in the sandy gravel by the creek, took his shirt off, and cupped water in his hands. Splashed his face, his head, and neck. He'd been sweating from working the drill, but that wasn't why he was burning up.

Rose had so much kindness and goodness stored up in her heart, the very things he didn't have and yet craved. She drew him like the inexorable attraction of a flower to a bee. He couldn't resist her before, and now she'd offered him the ultimate temptation.

*Love*.

No matter how desperately he wanted it, he couldn't take

it because he didn't deserve it. He'd let her down just as he'd let everyone down. The very fact that he married her proved he was selfish as well as rash. He destroyed the lives he touched. She couldn't see that because her infatuation blinded her.

Even after he'd told her the truth, she still wanted him.

The burning spread up his throat and into his eyes. A drop of water rolled off the end of his nose and splashed into the creek, and then another. He slapped cool water on his face and mopped it with his sleeve. Why had God or Fate brought them together? Was Providence testing him?

*"You have to be willing to let love do its work."*

Val stared at his shimmering reflection in the water. He'd tried to change and it hadn't worked. He'd never thought about love being able to change him and didn't have enough experience with it to know whether such a thing could be possible. He couldn't think of anyone who'd offered love after he'd hurt them. But that was what Rose had done.

*Love covers a multitude of sins.*

Dear God, he wanted to believe it was true, but he feared trusting in something he didn't understand. Love was an ephemeral emotion, a dream that had eluded him all his life. He wouldn't even know what it felt like to be loved except for Rose.

Even if her love could heal him, what could he do for her? If he tried to love and failed, what then? It would confirm the thing he feared most about himself. That he was incapable of love.

But if he didn't take the chance he would forever know he was something worse.

A coward.

## ❧ 16 ☙

While Val escaped to the creek, ostensibly to wash up for dinner, Rose sought refuge in the shanty. She stood inside, hugging her arms, struggling to hold back tears. She'd been grief-stricken and in soul-deep pain after losing her family. Even then, she hadn't felt this hopeless.

She had done everything she knew to do. Offered Val everything she had. If that wasn't enough, if he couldn't accept her love and love her in return, she had to let go and release him.

An unbearable ache welled in her chest, forcing out a harsh sob. She fought to hold back the flood. No more crying. Tears wouldn't help either of them. Keeping busy, though, would keep her mind off the inevitable.

Rose rummaged through the boxes, looking for bowls or something to hold soup. All she could come up with were two tin cups. They would have to do. The squatter who'd previously lived here must've taken most of his belongings, and Val hadn't thought he would be here long. Now that he'd found the coal, he'd want to sell out and leave as soon as possible. She wasn't sure he would go to England right away, but he'd made it clear he would leave without her.

She bit her lip at a pain that speared her chest. Now she understood why some people claimed they were dying from a broken heart. There was physical pain involved as well as mental and emotional anguish. Hurt seeped through every pore.

A high-pitched whinny came from outside.

Val had hobbled the horse out in the field, but that sounded close. Had the creature escaped or was Val hitching it up to leave? He wouldn't abandon her, no matter how angry or upset he might be.

Rose turned just as a shadow fell across the threshold and her heart caught in her throat.

Not Val. Jarvis. And he had a gun pointed at her.

Fear such as she had never felt before sent a cold wave over her skin.

"Well, well...if it ain't the long drink of water. You come out here for a poke, beanpole?" His knowing smirk made her skin crawl.

"How did you get out of jail?" She couldn't believe the army would've released him.

"I got friends."

"Mr. Childers?"

Jarvis snorted with a sound of derision. "Huh. He's scared of his own shadow." The unwavering gun preceded the intruder inside. His eyes never left her. "Where's your man?"

She considered throwing the cups to distract the gunman, then running for the wagon to see if Val had left his gun under the seat.

Jarvis drew back the hammer with a click. "Don't even think about tryin' anything."

The evil man was a mind reader or her face had given her away. She fought to school her features like Val could do when he didn't want anyone to know what he was thinking. Her pulse rushed in her ears, so loud she was sure Jarvis could hear it.

She had to distract him. Delay him while she listened for Val, and figure out a way to warn her husband. "It's not very gentlemanly to hold a gun on a lady."

He snorted. "You ain't no lady. And I ain't a gentleman."

"I am a lady, but I agree you are no gentleman." Rose squared her shoulders and held his disdainful gaze. Her father's words came back to her.

*Bullies are cowards, Rose. They'll bluster and try to scare you, but you look 'em in the eye like you'll take no guff and they'll back down.*

Jarvis sneered. "Don't get uppity on me, bitch. I asked you a question. Where's your man?"

"He's gone."

"He ain't gone far. I saw the horse...and the coal." Jarvis's eyes glittered with greed. "Remind me to thank him for doin' the work. Makes it easier for me to get the reward."

So, he planned to murder Val and thought he could somehow take back the land.

Rose's skin heated with fury. Good. Hot anger was better than cold terror. She gripped the cups. They were probably useless, but at the moment they were the only weapons she had, other than her hands and feet. "The only reward you'll get is waiting for you in hell."

In the blink of an eye, he'd grabbed her by her hair. Gasping, she opened her hands to fight him off and dropped the tin cups. With a jerk, he dragged her head down, pressing the barrel of the gun to her forehead. "Tell me where he is!"

Her stomach heaved. Had she eaten anything, it would've come up. As it was, her mouth filled with a bitter, coppery taste. She stammered the only thing she could think of. "He-he's gone to retrieve his hat. I don't know where he left it."

Jarvis made a grunt that sounded like displeasure. His nostrils flared and his sparse mustache twitched, reminding her of a sewer rat sniffing the air for food...or danger. Looking into his dark eyes was like looking into the eyes of one of those foul creatures. His tight grip on her hair pulled at her scalp and hurt, but she didn't dare move for fear he'd pull the trigger.

Her skin grew chilled and damp. "Please, let go of my hair."

He twisted his hold tighter. "Where's the deed?"

"I don't know." That truth came out easily.

With surprising strength, he hauled her to the table and slammed her head down.

Her forehead struck the surface and pain splintered behind her eyes. She cried out, scrabbling for something to hold onto as her vision blurred. Her fingers found the table edge and she clung to it, dizzy, legs trembling.

When she'd been little, she would close her eyes so the monsters couldn't see her. This monster wouldn't go away. Shutting everything out left Val with no one to help him. She turned her face toward the door, blinking at the light, forcing her mind to focus. Thoughts darted through her head like startled rabbits. She couldn't follow any of them.

"Rose!" Val's frantic yell pierced the veil of terror. Her mind captured a terrifying thought. That was Jarvis's plan, to bring Val to her so he could shoot him.

She screamed out a warning. "Gun!"

"Shut up!" The hard barrel pressed into her temple and her captor's fetid breath blew hot against her cheek. "Make another sound or so much as twitch that ass and I'll plant a bullet in your brain."

Rose struggled to breathe past the fear clamping her

throat closed. She couldn't let Val walk into a trap. This man planned to kill him, and her as well. If one of them had to die, she would rather it be her. Though if that happened, Val would take on more guilt and self-hatred.

Something appeared in the doorway. A shadow, then a flash of white.

Jarvis jerked the gun from her head. The explosion made her ears ring. Acrid smoke filled her nostrils. She choked on it.

Her heart ceased beating. Jarvis had shot Val.

*No, no, no...*

Mad with grief, she twisted around, clawing at the devil, not caring if she lived or died.

Jarvis swore as her nails found his face and left four fiery trails across his cheek. He pulled the gun back. The click of the hammer sounded like a death knell.

Someone streaked into the room, barreling into her tormenter. His gun went off with a loud crack, a flash and more smoke. But nothing slowed his shirtless attacker who carried him into the wall of crates with a crash.

Cans flew into the air.

Dizzy, Rose braced her arms, using the table to support her. For a moment it looked like four men were grappling for control of the gun. She stared, dazed and disbelieving.

Val had survived, and he'd come to her rescue with a vengeance.

She tried to stand so she could go to him, help him, but her legs had turned into noodles.

Jarvis, flat on his back, flailing like a roach, slammed the gun up against Val's head, causing him to lurch to one side. Jarvis didn't get the chance to do it again.

Val grabbed his wrist and twisted violently. With a screech, Jarvis dropped the weapon.

Coming to his feet, Val swayed. After gaining his balance,

he grabbed Jarvis's shirt and dragged the man up, out of the broken crates and scattered cans, and delivered a walloping punch to the man's face. It made a sickening, bone-crunching sound.

Jarvis crumpled to the floor and didn't move.

Val hunched over him, hands fisted, his back and shoulders moving as his breathing came in harsh rasps. He bent down and scooped up the gun, curled his finger around the trigger, and studied the weapon as if considering using it before tucking it into the back of his waistband.

Rose released a pent-up breath. She cried out his name, stiffened her legs, and wobbled into his arms. He caught her just before she collapsed. Lifting her, he carried her to the bed and gently laid her on the blanket. He knelt beside her, his beloved face hovering over her, taut with concern.

He gently pulled at strands of hair stuck to her throbbing forehead. "You're bleeding." His voice dipped low with emotion. "I should've been here."

"I'm glad you weren't." She glanced over at the unconscious man and began trembling. "He...he was looking for the deed. He wanted to kill you."

"I heard you cry out, and the warning about the gun." Anguish darkened her husband's eyes. "Put my shirt on the broomstick to give him something to shoot at. After he fired and thought he hit me, I knew he'd let down his guard."

Her husband's quick thinking had saved both their lives.

Recalling the moment she'd thought he was dead brought on a rush of scalding tears. She lightly touched the side of his head where he'd been hit with the gun. He winced.

"You're hurt," she choked out.

Val grasped her hand. "I'm fine. But we need to get you to a doctor. Give me a moment to tie up this piece of trash, then I'll take you into town."

Rose darted a fearful look at their attacker. Had he

moved? It didn't look like it. But her mind formed a terrifying image of Jarvis rising and attacking them again. Like a frightened child, she clung to Val's hand. "Don't leave me."

He brought the back of her hand to his lips in a fervent kiss. "Never."

"Val, ye don't have to carry me. I can walk." Despite Rose's objection, her husband scooped her into his arms and carried her downstairs as if she weighed no more than a feather.

She circled her arms around his neck, still amazed by his strength. "I did manage to get dressed this morning without your help."

"Not used to being pampered like a fine lady, eh?" His mouth kicked up in a teasing half-smile. "We need to practice more."

Ever since he'd rushed her back to town to see a doctor, he'd insisted on carting her everywhere, as well as dressing—and undressing—her. He curled up beside her in bed at night, holding her close, soothing her when she woke, crying out and trembling.

The night terrors weren't as frequent or intense as they'd been the first few nights, true to the doctor's prediction. He'd said her mind would heal as the injury to her head healed, and he had given her medicine. But it was Val's tender care that did the most good.

Val carried her into the parlor where Charm, Delilah, and Susannah sat, reading and sewing. The three had taken turns sitting with her during the days she'd been on strict bed rest.

"Rose, dear, it's good to see you up and around." Susannah vacated the sofa, taking with her the trousers she'd been mending. Danny's, based on the size. She draped a knitted throw over the arm of the couch. "Wrap this around your shoulders so you won't get chilled."

"Chilled?" The weather had turned warm and Rose tended to be hot-blooded. "I've been keeping my window open at night to let in a breeze. I'm roasting."

"We can't have you roasting. I'll find you a fan." Val settled her on the bolstered seat. With the careful way he handled her, one might think she was fragile as glass.

As much as she loved his attention, it made her worry about his motive.

He'd declared the entire incident was his fault, which it wasn't. Every time she tried to argue with him about it, he told her quarreling would hinder healing.

They *would* talk about it now that she'd been released from her feather-mattress prison.

He kissed the top of her head before he set off in search of a fan.

After he was gone, Charm closed the book in her lap. She'd taken off her shoes and tucked her legs underneath her mint-green skirt, curled up in the chair like a child. Her behavior flouted what would be deemed acceptable, but she somehow managed to get away with it because she looked so innocent. Charm might be as tiny and adorable as a child, but her naiveté was an act.

"He's become domesticated," she observed with amusement twinkling in her luminous brown eyes. She twirled a golden curl. "Does he jump when you crook your finger?

Growing too warm, Rose removed the shawl Val had

wrapped around her shoulders and laid it next to the throw. "Don't let him fool you. He's just doing his penance."

"That ought to take a while...sixty, seventy years," Susannah murmured.

Rose knew her friend was joking, but she felt compelled to defend her husband. "Val saved my life."

"Yes, he did. He acted very bravely, and he has taken good care of you. I'll admit I've warmed up to him," Susannah said.

"I'm getting hungry," Delilah put her embroidery on her lap. "Has your appetite returned, Rose?"

"Somewhat. Val made sure I didn't starve."

For a few days, she'd been too sick to eat. Val had coaxed Prudence into cooking whatever appealed to Rose. One day she'd craved a bite of the Irish stew her mother used to make. Prudence had replicated it almost perfectly.

"Mrs. Fry said she would serve sandwiches in the dining room as soon as the other ladies are done interviewing their suitors," Susannah remarked.

*Interviewing?* That made it sound like they were hiring help.

"You mean socializing," Rose corrected.

Susannah didn't look up from her sewing. "Yes, of course."

"How is it going?" Rose was almost afraid to ask. When she'd left the Lagonda House, none of the other women had been close to accepting proposals.

Mr. Hardt's patience had to be reaching an end.

"Two more marriages were announced this week. Faster than I expected." Susannah finally looked up from the mending in her lap and made a disgruntled face. "That's not fast enough for Mr. Hardt. I suspect he would've thrown us into the streets if it weren't for your injury."

Rose didn't believe the railroad agent to be as callous as he'd first seemed. But she wouldn't convince Susannah.

Maybe it wasn't just Val or Mr. Hardt she distrusted. Men in general were the problem.

"I have some good news," Charm announced. "You'll be happy to know that Mr. Jarvis will be charged with attempted murder and face trial—after his fractured wrist and broken jaw heal." Her lips curved in a satisfied smile. "He won't be in any condition to bother women for a long time."

Rose didn't feel pleased or amused, only relieved. "I never want to see that awful man's face again."

Charm's smile faded. "I suppose you'll have to see him when you testify in court."

Rose pulled her mother's shawl around her shoulders, not for warmth but for the comfort it brought. "I hadn't thought about that."

"Don't be afraid. Just tell the court what he did to you," Susannah advised. "If there's any justice in this world, they'll lock him up and throw away the key."

Delilah shook her head. "Jailing him isn't enough. That low-down skunk deserves to hang for what he did to you!"

The fierce outburst came as something of a surprise from the soft-spoken belle. As she gazed at Rose with sympathetic anguish in her eyes, her hand drifted to her marred cheek.

The scar might've come from something other than an accident. Whatever had happened, Delilah hadn't seen justice served.

Rose gingerly touched her forehead. If Jarvis escaped again, he might come after her and do worse than smash her head against a table. But if he got away with it because she was afraid to testify, he would be free to hurt other women. "I'll face him in court and testify."

"Brave lass!" Charm clapped for her.

Rose didn't feel brave. The cut on her head required stitches and would leave a scar. She'd been assured it would fade, but she'd been horrified when she looked into a mirror.

Purplish red bruises had darkened to almost black, even spreading around her eyes.

Val had tried to comfort her. He'd insisted a scar wouldn't diminish her beauty. Rather, it would add character. He'd even joked about the "rainbow" across her forehead as being a sign from God that nothing bad would happen to her again. And if the Almighty slipped up, her husband would be at her side to make sure she remained safe.

But he hadn't said he loved her.

Misery dropped like a rock to the pit of her stomach.

From what she'd learned about her husband, she feared he might commit his life to her out of guilt or a sense of obligation. He had enough of those burdens to bear. Even if he reached the point where he forgave himself for his past sins, he didn't want to build a life out here. And she'd been fooling herself to think she could fit into his world, no matter how long she practiced being a fine lady. He knew it too. He'd always known this, but he'd been too considerate to come right out and say it. No, as much as it hurt, she had to let him go. As soon as he returned, she would take him aside and tell him so.

As if her thoughts had called to him, he appeared.

The ladies greeted him, then they all came up with some excuse to leave the room.

"Do you think it's me?" he asked after they'd exited.

Rose supposed her friends had decided she ought to have time alone with her husband. "No, they like you."

"It's not them I'm trying to impress." He held a long roll of paper under one arm and something else in his other hand, which he presented with a flourish. "Your fan, milady."

Rose opened the delicate item. It was made from ivory lace painted with pink rosebuds. She turned it in her hand, admiring it. "It's so pretty. Where did you get it?"

"Mr. Middaugh has expanded his selection of ladies'

accessories."

Val had gone out and purchased an expensive fan without her even asking for one.

Amazed, Rose hardly knew what to say. "You went all the way to the store?"

"The store is only a block away, and I have long legs, which I assume you've noticed." His suggestive smile set loose a flurry of wings in her stomach.

She couldn't stop her gaze from dropping past his red and gold brocade vest to the creased black trousers concealing what she knew to be two very long, very nice legs. He'd draped one over her at some point the previous night. She'd been tempted to invite him to snuggle even closer. Her mouth grew dry as the fluttery sensations moved lower.

Rose jerked the fan to her heated face. "Thank you, it's perfect."

"Does this make me a *bene cove?*" Val asked her.

She stopped fanning and peered over the top. "Where did you hear that?"

He sat beside her and laid the rolled paper across his knees. "Last night, when you said, *be a bene cove, love, and open the window.*"

Had she said it in her sleep? She didn't remember.

Rose gave him a cheeky smile. "Not just a *bene cove*, a good man, I'd say you're a *benen cove*, a better man."

"Better, eh? My competitive nature won't settle for anything less than the best. I'll have to keep trying."

He probably meant it as a joke. But based on what he'd revealed about his childhood, she knew he had never felt as though he could do enough. Her heart yearned to pour out her affection in words, as well as kisses and caresses.

She stroked his cheek before she kissed him. "Just be you," she said softly. "That's good enough for me."

His gaze hung on hers, searching, questioning.

Did he doubt her? He didn't have to dote on her or spoil her. All he had to do was love her. This, though, seemed to be the one thing he couldn't give. She couldn't force him to feel something he didn't, and he hadn't married her for love.

She touched the fan to his arm. "Would you go outside with me? I need some fresh air after being stuck in bed for a week."

He looked a bit chagrined. "Of course, I'd be happy to take you out. After I return. I have an appointment with Mr. Hardt first."

The last thing Val needed was another confrontation.

"Oh, dear. What has he done now?"

Her husband reacted with a rueful smile. "He's done nothing. Yet. I hope he might be interested enough in my plans to make introductions." Val tapped the rolled paper on his knee. "The land should be worth a great deal to someone interested in mining all that coal."

Rose drew the fan through her fingers to hide the tremble. "You still wish to sell."

"For the right price. If it's worth what I think it is, we'll have more than enough to live on." He touched her cheek with his fingertips and gave her a light kiss. "I'll buy you all the fans you want."

So, he had promised not to leave her and he would keep his word. That's what he meant.

Rose's eyes burned. She longed to stay with him more than anything. But not because he'd made a promise in a moment of weakness. "Go on then, talk to Mr. Hardt, and when you come back, we'll go for a walk."

Val stood and tucked the paper under his arm. "Better yet, I'll bring a buggy around and take you for a ride."

She stretched out one leg, and with a smile drew back her skirt to reveal an ankle. "Oh, I'd prefer to walk. I have two very long legs, as I'm sure you've noticed."

## ❧ 18 ❧

While Hardt examined his drawings, Val sat in the chair across from the railroad agent's desk and drummed his fingers on his knees. He started to reach for his pocket watch then thought better of it. That would make him appear too anxious.

He let his mind drift to the previous moments with Rose. She'd shown him a pretty ankle, with that saucy smile. He'd considered tossing the drawing aside, sweeping her into his arms, and carrying her upstairs. But then, as now, he'd forced himself to exercise patience.

Once he was certain her injury had healed, he would find a private place where he could properly seduce his wife. Or she could seduce him. He'd be fine with that too.

Hardt sat back with a straight face. "Why are you showing me these drawings?"

He was joking, right? Or he didn't understand what he was looking at.

Val came out of the chair and propped his hand on the desk. He pointed to a sketch he'd made of the type of mines he'd recommend based on the likely quantity of coal beneath the ground. "Here is where to sink shafts. This shows the placement of room-and-pillar sections. That's what these rectangles represent. It's a better process for mining the maximum amount of coal. I've estimated what might be produced in the first year, based on how soon the mine could be in operation, given the appropriate level of investment. A crew could be pulling coal out of the first section within a month."

The railroad agent glanced down at the drawings. He sat back in his chair and crossed his arms over his chest. "How is your wife feeling?"

"Much better, thank you."

"Have you made any plans about what you'll do?"

Val tensed. What was Hardt implying?  "I'll be taking Rose with me."

The gleam in Hardt's eyes might've been amusement in someone with a sense of humor. "That's good to hear."

"Now that we've established Rose's marital status, what are your thoughts about the mine?"

"We're in the business of running a railroad, not a mine."

Val searched Hardt's enigmatic expression. Perhaps the agent thought feigning disinterest would result in a lower price for the property. "The railroad uses coal. A great deal of it. They could operate a mine and pay less for fuel. I've done the survey, and checked samples. There's a very large deposit. No telling how deep it goes until you get down there, but I'd wager you'll pull out thousands of tons, if not millions before the mine is exhausted."

At this, Hardt leaned forward with an expression of interest. "How do you know so much about coal mining, Mr. Valentine?"

Perhaps Hardt believed he was being swindled. Val straightened and his face heated. What did he expect? He was a gambler, as far Hardt knew. Thus, the railroad agent's concern was reasonable. "My grandfather owned mines in Northumberland. Coal was the source of our family's wealth. I made it my business to learn what I could."

Val didn't add that he'd hoped to take over management of his family's concerns. He'd squandered that chance. But he wanted to repay his father for what the Baron had spent to bail him and his younger brother out of trouble. He intended to speak to Rose about it, although he already knew what she would say. She had the most generous heart of anyone he'd ever known.

"I have samples, and I've drawn up detailed plans. All I need is the right introduction. An investor with the railroad. One of the owners. A member of the board. Whoever you think might be interested."

Hardt stood and walked to the door, retrieving his hat.

What the hell was he doing?

Val frowned, having a little more trouble keeping his temper in check. "Are you tired of this conversation? Or have I offended you—beyond punching you in the face?"

"Neither." The railroad agent turned as he secured his hat. "I understand why you hit me. And I might've done the same had I walked in on a man holding hands with my wife—if I had a wife. No, I'm putting on another hat."

"Another hat?"

Hardt's expression remained placid. Almost pleasant. "Set aside for a moment the fact that I'm with the railroad. Assume I'm interested in helping you and your wife. Do you have an uncle?"

*An uncle?*

This meeting had taken a bizarre twist.

Val played along. He had no idea where Hardt was going, but it would become clear at some point. Hopefully. "Yes, I have an uncle. He and I despise each other."

Hardt propped his hip on the corner of his desk and

crossed his arms. "All right, just go along with me here. Let's agree that I am not speaking to you as a representative of the railroad. I'm speaking to you as Ross Hardt."

Whomever that man might be. He could be enjoying a joke or playing some cruel trick or doing something entirely incomprehensible...like being nice.

Val sank into his chair. Whatever the purpose, he could employ a little patience. "Very well. What do you have to say to me?"

"This town, this country, needs men like you. Educated, with good judgment, integrity, and courage. In short, gentlemen."

Val leaned back in amazement. Ross Hardt had just complimented him more with one sentence than his father had in all the speeches the Baron had delivered throughout his son's life. "I am not sure I heard you correctly.

Hardt did something else odd. He smiled. "I am asking you to consider staying. Open the mine and operate it. Based on this—" Hardt motioned to the drawings. "I'd say you have a solid plan, along with the background and knowledge."

*Stay here?* Val shook his head. He had to go back and make some attempt to repair the damage he'd done even if he couldn't erase the past. But why was Ross Hardt taking a personal interest in changing his mind? "If you're concerned about Rose, as I said, I plan to take her with me to England."

Hardt rubbed his chin thoughtfully. "What does she say about that?"

"We haven't discussed it at length."

"How do you think she'll get along with your family?"

Val braced his hands on his knees. This *uncle* nonsense had gone on long enough. "What is your interest in Rose?"

"Not what you think. She reminds me of my sister."

The brusque agent who'd been ready to dispose of women through a lottery had a sister?

"That's astounding," Val said.

"What's astounding?"

"You have a sister and yet know so little about women."

"You are married," Hardt shot back. "Yet you appear to know very little about your wife."

Val kept his hands glued to his knees. He would not hit this man, no matter how tempting. "What could you possibly know about Rose?"

Hardt's expression softened. "I know that she's none of my business. But I urge you to ask yourself, will she fit in with your family?"

*No.*

Val didn't voice the answer. Hardt's purpose wasn't to learn it but to challenge him to consider Rose's best interests.

Had this been Mr. Hardt's intention all along?

Val came to his feet and made a solemn bow. "It appears I owe you two apologies."

"If you believe so, I accept them."

The offended party didn't belabor the point. Val had nothing more to add, but Mr. Hardt seemed to be waiting for something else.

"Do you have a better offer in England?" he asked.

"Not a better offer. An obligation." Val hesitated, not sure he wanted to share something so personal even though he'd accepted that Hardt was being decent. "My family, I need to make..." *Retribution.* "Provision." That was his pride talking. "I owe them a debt."

"Does this debt involve more than money?"

*Money.* That sounded crass. But money was all his family would care to have from him. Any idea they might welcome him back with open arms was foolish imaginings. The sooner he accepted that, the better.

"No, nothing but money."

"Then why not repay them from what you earn out of the

mining operation?"

"Are we back to that again?" Val released a sardonic laugh. "I don't have the resources to open a mine, much less operate one."

Ross Hardt removed his "other hat" and placed it on the desk. Did this mean he was back to being the land agent? "The railroad has resources. I'll send a letter to the directors. In the meantime, I can arrange a personal loan to get you started."

Val stared at the drawings on the table. He had no excuse or escape this time. If he wanted to do something with his life, here was his chance. But he had to risk that he might not be any good at it.

What would Rose say? She'd tell him he could do it. Because she believed in him, he might be able to believe in himself.

In return for his liberality, Hardt would want something. Val was in no position to refuse. "You wish to be a partner?"

Hardt shook his head. "Not a partner. I don't want to become that involved."

"I'll give you a percentage of the business. I insist."

"Fine, then. We'll come to an agreement that's fair for both of us."

Val couldn't quite fathom what had just happened, except he felt sure he'd been granted some sort of miracle. He just hadn't expected it to come from this quarter.

He held out his hand. "I agree and extend my gratitude."

Hardt grasped Val's outstretched hand, the first time he'd done so. "Excellent. I take it to mean you're staying?"

"If Rose agrees, and I believe she'll be pleased. I know she likes it here."

"Then I think a drink is in order." Hardt went behind the desk and retrieved a bottle and two glasses from a drawer. "Whiskey?"

"Thank you."

Hardt held up his glass. "Here's to your new venture."

"We'll drink to the..." Val hesitated. "I'll need to name the mine."

"Call it Valentine's Rose." Hardt clinked the glasses together.

Another surprising revelation. The dour man had a sentimental streak.

"I should've thought of that," Val muttered. He took a sip. "This is smooth." Too smooth. "After a few drinks, I won't remember what we called it."

Hardt's mouth pulled into a sly smile. "Maybe I should offer Mrs. Braddock some of my whiskey so she'll stop interfering." His brows drew together in a look of puzzlement. "Wonder why she came out here? She's not acting like she wants to be married."

Ross Hardt had business sense, and even a smattering of sentimentality, but he was hopeless when it came to women. He'd made an enemy of the one person who could help him most.

Val shifted forward. "Let me offer you a suggestion. Put Mrs. Braddock in charge of matchmaking. Better still, *hire* her as a matchmaker. Then she'll be compelled to prove she's capable. I predict it will speed up the process considerably."

"Hire her?" Hardt snorted. "What makes you think I want her working for me?"

Val shrugged. "Why not? She's a natural leader, has the respect of the other women, and she likes to be in charge. She'd be perfect for the job." Val set down his glass. He picked up his drawings and rolled them into a tube. "You have to admit, you're terrible at matchmaking."

Hardt finished off his drink. "Oh, I don't know. I did a fair job setting you up with Rose."

## ❧ 19 ❧

Three hours later, Val brought a buggy around, just as he'd promised. Rose insisted on walking outside, but she allowed him to help her up into the seat. He took the reins and turned the horse around, heading out of town.

"Where are we going?"

"I thought we might ride out to the property. There's something I want to show you."

"You found a buyer." She tried to sound happy for him.

"Not exactly."

She didn't know what he meant by that, but it didn't matter. The time had come to tell him he didn't have to worry about her any longer, that as soon as he sold his land, he could go, and God speed. At least, those were the lines she'd rehearsed. Saying them was another thing entirely. "When...when will you return to England?"

He glanced over at her, reproachful. "You're spoiling my surprise."

"I didn't realize that was a surprise."

"Not that. You'll see."

The day had turned out to be perfect, warm, with a nice breeze, unless one was riding in a buggy behind a fast-trotting horse. She reached up to tighten the ribbon beneath her chin so her opera bonnet wouldn't fly off in the wind. "This horse is fast."

"Not nearly as fast as the ones I prefer to ride."

"Remind me never to ride with you."

"I'll purchase a gentle horse for you."

Rose hugged her shawl closer. He'd opened the door for a conversation about the future. She'd put it off as long as possible. "Val, I want you to know how much I appreciate all you've done for me. You've been a kind, attentive, caring husband."

He arched a brow at her. "Have you confused me with someone else? I've been terrible to you, except these past few days, which doesn't make up for my previous ill-treatment."

"Don't be silly. You haven't treated me ill, and you saved my life. You're *good-wooled*."

"Good what?"

"*Good-wooled*. Means you've got courage and don't flinch."

He smiled a pleased smile. "Sweet Rose. I love your colorful adjectives."

She had no idea what that was, but the fact that he loved something about her eased some of her misgivings. Maybe she was wrong about his motive. Her heart beat faster.

"Do you love more than my, er, adjectives?"

He burst out with a laugh. Had she said something funny? "Oh yes, the list of things I love about you is much longer."

The tiny flicker of hope burned brighter. "Will you tell me what's on it, this list?"

He turned the horse down the road she'd traveled when she'd come out to see him. The wheels dropped into a rut, sending her sliding across the seat. He lifted his arm and brought her closer. "On my list of what I love about Rose

Muldoon Valentine: your height, a perfect fit to mine, your lovely elegant hands, your *long* legs...."

She blushed as he eyed said limbs with a knowing smile.

"Your pretty blushes, smooth skin, sweet lips..."

Rose sighed. "Aye, I love your lips too."

"My turn first. Then you can list all the things you love about me."

She bit her lip, smiling.

"Let's see, where was I? Oh yes, more body parts are on the list, but I think I'll wait until we're alone so I can pay special attention to each one of them."

And she would return the favor. But not until she'd established the reason he'd changed his mind after telling her he didn't want her love.

"Do you still think it's your fault, what happened?"

He was silent for a moment. "I do blame myself because Jarvis wouldn't have hurt you if you hadn't been with me."

"Are you keeping me because you feel obliged?"

"What?" He slowed the horse and turned onto the path. The tall grass slapped at the sides of the buggy as they headed toward the homestead. "Haven't you heard anything I've said?"

"Your list, you mean? It's nice, yes."

He drew back on the reins until the horse came to a halt, and then turned to her, frowning. "Nice? I'm telling you I love you. That's more than *nice*."

She searched his earnest face, afraid to believe. "You...love me?"

"You sound surprised. Have I done such a poor job of showing it?"

"No, you've been so good to me, spoiling me. But I thought you were doing it because you felt guilty about what happened. And, you told me you didn't want my love."

He gathered her hands, looking down at them, rubbing

his thumb over hers, as if he couldn't bear to look at her. But then he did, and his eyes were very bright. "That was a lie. I need your love, Rose. I crave it. But...I was afraid I couldn't love you like you deserve to be loved, and that I would disappoint you."

"Oh Val, you never—"

He put his finger to her lips, silencing her. "I know. You don't seem to see the things that are wrong with me. Or maybe you do and, as you said, you don't care. You told me I needed to let love do its work, and that's what I'm willing to do...if you'll give me the chance."

Replacing his finger with his lips, he gave her a reverent kiss. "Marry me, Rose. Be my wife in every way. Teach me how to love. That's what I love best about you. Your heart."

Rose went into his arms, laughing. Pure joy welled up and spilled over. "I love you, Val, and I'll marry you as many times as you want."

She hugged her husband, and he hugged her in return, and they kissed and hugged and kissed some more. At last, she laid her head on his shoulder and knew she would never know more happiness, or if she did, it would be with him.

"What is the surprise you're wanting to show me?"

"Just this." He reached behind the seat and withdrew the rolled paper then spread them out on his lap. "These are drawings for a mine. Mr. Hardt has kindly offered to loan me the funds to get started and to introduce me to other potential investors."

"What does that mean?"

"It means we'll be staying here, Rose. I'll be opening a mine and operating it. We'll eventually have enough to build a very nice home—out here or in town, it's your choice."

Rose gazed wonderingly at the tall grass around them, imagining a cozy cottage in place of the tarpaper shack. She'd plant daisies out front and a vegetable garden in the back.

The nearby creek and wide-open prairie would be Nature's playground. Their children wouldn't walk through sewage-filled streets or sleep in crowded tenements and breathe fetid air.

Joyful tears coursed down her cheeks. "'Tis a perfect place to have a home. But what made you change your mind about going back to England?"

"Besides falling in love with you?" He tweaked her nose and a smile lifted one side of his mouth. "I realized there was no point to going back. You were right. I can't change the past or what I did. I can only try to live a better life now. I plan to give my father and my brothers a share in the mine. If you agree. They may never want to see me again, but this is something I need to do."

"Of course, whatever you think is the right thing." She reached up and stroked his cheek. "What are their names, your brothers?"

"Julius and Hadrian."

"Constantine, Julius, and Hadrian," Rose said with a smile. "They sound very important."

Val made a face. "My father wanted to name his sons after Roman emperors. He fancied creating a dynasty."

"Roman emperors? I heard they were bad."

"There were some bad apples. Constantine converted. He brought Christianity to the empire so I suppose he did some good."

Did Val realize what it meant? Probably. He was smarter than her.

Rose slid her arm through his and leaned against her husband's shoulder. "So you're saying that men who've done bad things can turn around and do good and be remembered for those things?"

His smile started slow then spread. "Are you trying to teach me a lesson?"

She leaned over and kissed him. "Just telling you something you already know."

*Rose has found her true love, but what about the other women who answered the railroad advertisement to come west and seek husbands? Actress Charm LaBelle talks an Irish saloon owner into hiring her until she can escape her past. Marriage is not in the cards. But Lady Luck is about to change that. Start reading Patrick's Charm today.*

# MORE FROM E.E. BURKE

*Find out what happens to the other women who signed up with the railroad to come west in **The Bride Train Series.***

Valentine's Rose

Patrick's Charm

Tempting Prudence

Seducing Susannah

*Where did the bride lottery start? Book 1 in **Steam! Romance & Rails.** If you love dark deceits, daring heroes and scorching love stories, you'll adore this series.*

Her Bodyguard

Redbird

A Dangerous Passion

Fugitive Hearts

Not far from where **The Bride Train** takes place is the historic town of Fort Scott. Meet two shopkeepers who compete for more than business.

Victoria Bride of Kansas

Santa's Mail Order Bride

Also in Audible

Sign up for my newsletter for exclusive articles, and be the first to find out about special discounts and new releases. www.eeburke.com

# RESEARCH NOTES

My inspiration for *The Bride Train* series came from true events that took place in southeastern Kansas shortly after the Civil War. Immigration into the young state drew thousands of veterans seeking cheap land, as well as swindlers who were eager to take advantage of the chaotic land grab. Setters who staked claims under preemption rights were forced to broker deals with the railroad and disputes over ownership sparked riots. By 1869, President Grant had to send troops into Kansas to quell the violence.

While researching, I found a fascinating account about a creative solution to end the violence, which included importing single young ladies into Kansas to become brides. Their presence, it was argued, would provide a "calming influence" on the unruly men. I couldn't find evidence this program ever got off the ground, but it made for a great romance series.

The railroad-sponsored bride lottery program is first mentioned in my debut novel, *Her Bodyguard,* which is set against the same historical events, but in a different location. That scene inspired me to conceive an entire series about a railroad matchmaking service. The first question that popped into my head was, "What kind of woman would leave everything behind and go to an uncivilized land to marry virtual strangers?

Research for the first book led me to Five Points, a nineteenth-century slum in New York City that housed a large population of poor Irish immigrants. The descriptions of this slum were so awful it made me wonder why more people didn't leave. Crowded, unsanitary, and crime-ridden, but to the immigrants who lived there, it was home. For Rose Muldoon, an Irish laundress, it takes more than poverty to drive her away. After tragedy strikes, she leaves behind the familiar and ventures into the unknown, longing to replace the family she's lost and find a place to belong.

During this same era, England's noblest families were sending their sons to America to toughen them up, hoping these second sons, who wouldn't inherit land and title, might make their fortunes elsewhere, or at least make something meaningful of their dissolute lives. Constantine Valentine (Val) comes from an aristocratic background as far from Rose's world as the sun is from the moon.

The surname Valentine, of Anglo-Saxon origin, is from the Latin name *Valentinus*, from the root word *Valens*, which means strong and healthy. The word "valor" comes from this root. But even a strong man is bound to have a weakness. In Val's case, he suffers from what is known today as Attention-Deficit Disorder. Being misunderstood and ridiculed for his impetuous nature has a devastating impact on his life, and it takes a special woman with a great capacity for love to help Val overcome his past.

*E.E. Burke*

# ABOUT THE AUTHOR

E.E. Burke's historical romances combine her unique blend of wit and warmth. Her books have been nominated for numerous national and regional awards, including Book-sellers' Best, National Readers' Choice, and Kindle Best Book. She was also a finalist in the RWA's prestigious Golden Heart® contest. Over the years, she's been a disc jockey, a journalist, and an advertising executive, before finally getting around to living the dream--writing stories readers can get lost in.

Find out more about her books at her website: www. eeburke.com.

www.ingramcontent.com/pod-product-compliance
Lightning Source LLC
Chambersburg PA
CBHW070924130626
46555CB00001B/274